Highwayman: Ironside

Michael Arnold

PART ONE: THE CHASE

Beside Pruetts Lane, North of Petersfield, Hampshire,
November 1655

The storm was long spent, but its legacy lingered, the mud now deep and slick.

The horse's iron-tipped limbs slipped and scrabbled for purchase as it fought to maintain its gallop, scoring deep furrows through the lane's sunken, waterlogged belly. But still it forged on, snorting its efforts to the threatening clouds that scudded across the evening sky. It stumbled, whinnied wildly, squealing a plaintive cry that fell on deaf ears before gathering chaotic limbs in thunderous rhythm, guttural grunts pulsing steam that rose in roiling jets to briefly swallow its rider.

The rider pushed himself into the steed's billowing silver mane, the stench of horse flesh and sweat filling his nostrils. He touched his spurs to the dappled grey flanks. The horse snorted again, jerked its granite-hard neck in annoyance, eyes blazing white in the slate dusk. But it quickened all the same. The rider grinned.

A branch flashed into view like a low-flying gull, whipping out of the oppressive haze in a blur, sending the rider into a desperate crouch, hugging his mount's moist neck. They raced below its swiping range, relief pulsing atop each rasped out-breath, and the rider crowed his exhilaration into the dripping canopy, invigorated by the thrill of the chase. And there it was, suddenly and brilliantly, emerging from the hazy half-light like a wheeled ghost. His quarry.

The coach grew in size and definition, blooming a hundred yards off like the pall of smoke from a spark-touched bag of gunpowder. The rider held his breath, gritted his teeth till they ached, heart beating like a Naseby drum, scalp prickling, muscles tense. He revelled in the speed, in the danger, in the spray of mud and the eye-stinging air.

And then he was beside the clattering vehicle, veering to the left of the rear wheels. He took the reins in a single gloved palm and let his free hand drop, groping for the smooth handle of his pistol. There it was, jutting up from his saddle holster, the metal-bound butt hard and reassuring. He jerked it free, luxuriating in its brutish weight, and kicked again, the horse mustering a final burst of speed so that they drew up alongside the driver. The rider looked straight ahead, alert to the hazards of the road, but his arm swept out like a sailboat's boom to bring the pistol level with the coachman's head.

"Slow 'em up, cully, lest I clean your ear with lead!" From the corner of his eye he could see the coachman glance across at him. The thundering pair of bays harnessed out front did not falter. "Rein them in, friend!" he called again. "Do not make me kill you!"

The beasts whinnied as their harnesses pulled taut and, as though the mud had deepened in that instant to suck at the crashing fetlocks, the bays fell to a canter, to a trot, and finally walked to a steam-shrouded halt.

The rider wheeled his mount back to face the coach. It was a splendid thing indeed, like the jewellery box of a giant, half gold, half cornflower blue, the doors draped with patterned curtains of silver and black. He kept the pistol up, steady and level. "Jump down, there's a good fellow."

The driver dropped his reins. A musket lay on the timber platform at his feet, and he cast it a surreptitious glance.

"Do not be a dullard," the rider warned.

The coachman swallowed hard, nodded, and scrambled down to earth. He was a short, plump man, probably in his early forties, with warts on his chin and a syphilitic nose.

He snatched off his felt hat to reveal a patc of thinning brownish hair and nodded emphatically. "Don't kill me, sir, I beg you. I've four chil'ens and..."

"Away with you," the rider snapped. The terrified driver needed no further encouragement and bolted into the tree line, vanishing noisily amongst the safety of the undergrowth like a startled fawn. "You inside!" the rider called as he dismounted and strode up to the inert coach. "Out you come, and be sharp about it!"

Nothing moved. The bays whickered nervously as though they discussed their plight with the rider's big grey, but from the coach there came nothing but silence. The rider took a step nearer. "Do not be foolish," he called in a steady tone, "for you will not live to regret the mistake."

The coach swayed like a milkmaid's hips as someone moved inside, huge springs creaking noisily beneath, and he braced himself, one foot in front of the other like a man striding into a gale.

"I am stepping out!" a voice called from within the gilt shell. It rocked more vigorously.

The rider noted the depth of tone. The stentorian edge that made him think of his time with the cavalry. It made his neck prickle. "No weapons! Raise your hands where I may see them, and move slowly!"

"To whom am I speaking?" the voice barked back.

"Lyle!" the rider replied strongly, knowing the revelation could only serve to move matters along more swiftly.

The sticky earth trembled. More hoof beats. Lyle peered past the coach to see the approach of a black gelding and a roan mare. The black was ridden by a man wearing a buff coat that sagged across the shoulders to betray a painfully thin frame beneath. His face was creased deeply with age, fringed by a neat beard of wintry whiteness, and made severe by a long, hooked nose that was bright red at the tip. His neck convulsed in a violent twitch as he waved cheerily. "Shall I take the reins?"

"You'd better," Lyle snapped, irritation bubbling in his veins. "For you've done nought else of use this day."

The old man twitched again and grinned. "The branch wasn't long enough, Major, 'pon my life it was not." He slid down from the saddle and spread his palms. "A miscalculation is all."

"We'll discuss it later," Lyle said. "And cover your ugly face."

The old man flashed an amused sneer and drew a silken scarf up from his collar to envelope his head. A pair of holes had been cut in the material through which his blue eyes gleamed.

"He's right, Samson," the second newcomer said. The face was already masked, and the body clothed in the garments of a man, but her feminine voice seemed to jar against the deeper tones of the others.

Lyle looked up at the diminutive figure who deftly brought her powerful steed to a halt. She was twelve, they reckoned, but she might have been twenty, such was her confident bearing, and he suppressed a smile. "I said later. Now to your business."

She nodded, cocking a long pistol in one smooth, practised motion. "Let's see what's what, then."

"I have placed my pistols inside!" the voice from within the coach announced.

"Let us see you then, sir," Lyle replied.

After a brief pause the curtain at the small door was swept aside and a head poked out into the chill evening air. The man had seen perhaps fifty winters. He had a broad, ruddy face and straight grey hair sprouting from beneath the rim of a wide, feathered hat. His eyes were dark and bright with intelligence, and his lips thin - pressed into a hard line. He ducked back for an instant, a clunk announced the door's catch had been freed, and it swung outward. The man edged out like a rat easing from its hole, a rotund torso and short legs emerging in turn. He wore the

8

attire of a soldier - a suit of oiled buff hide and metal - but one of high rank, for the shapes cut out of his rapier's guard were ostentatiously intricate, and his coat was lined with golden thread.

Lyle sighed. "Stone me for a base rogue if there isn't a guard for even the smallest carriage these dull days!"

The elderly man who had gone to take the reins of the mud-spattered bays gave a wet-sounding cackle. "As if the roads ain't safe, Major."

Lyle glanced quickly back at him. "Quite so, Mister Grumm, quite so!" He returned his gaze to the well-upholstered fellow who now stood with his back pressed against one of the coach's big wheels. "But what exactly is he guarding?"

The armoured fellow squared his shoulders and widened his stance, standing like a sentinel before the coach. "I protect a man whose boots you are not fit so much as to lick, sir."

Lyle trained the firearm at his face. "I will decide that, sir. And if I must blast a hole 'twixt your eyeballs to do it then I am ready and willing." He saw the man eye the pistol with interest and twitched the twin muzzles a touch. "She's Dutch. You like her?"

"What manner of weapon is it?"

"A flintlock as you'd know it, sir," Lyle said, "though she has a pair of barrels mounted 'pon an axle pin. So I may choose to shoot each of your stones out in turn, should you give me cause."

"What do you want?" the voice of another man broke the tension. It was slightly muffled, coming from within the vehicle, but not so much that Lyle could mistake the rounded notes of an East Anglian accent. "I say, Walmsley! What does the blackguard want?"

The guard, Walmsley, kept his gaze fixed upon the poised firearm. "He wants you to fear him, sir. This is the infamous Samson Lyle." He spat. "The *Ironside Highwayman*."

Lyle touched a finger to the brim of his hat. "At your service. Though the name is not something I encourage. A creation of the news sheets, I'm afraid."

The curtain crumpled suddenly and was thrust aside. Out of the coach stepped a man in simple black breeches and doublet, with a tall buckled hat and tidy falling band collar. To Lyle's eyes he was dressed like a puritan preacher, except that the clothes were stretched so tightly over his corpulent midriff that such an austere vocation seemed unlikely. Besides, Lyle knew from the accent that he had found his man and he inwardly thanked God for it.

10

"Ah ah ah," Lyle warned as he noticed Walmsley's hand snake to the small of his back. He twitched the pistol in his grip. "What have you hidden there?" The guard's jaw quivered. "Ground arms, my man, or you'll find yourself staring at the clouds."

Slowly Walmsley eased a small pistol from his belt and let it drop to the ground. "I have no more, save my blade."

Lyle nodded. "Try any more tricks, and things will go badly for you." He winked. "There's a good fellow."

"You are a bastardly gullion, Lyle," Walmsley growled.

Lyle gave a weary sigh. "Bark when you have teeth, sir. For now, mine is the only bite that matters." He looked beyond the soldier to the plainly attired passenger. "Let me see you, sir."

The fat fellow stepped tentatively to the side, though he remained firmly behind his bodyguard. "You know this man, Walmsley?"

"Every military man knows him, sir," Walmsley replied. "A soldier, as was. A good one. A good man, no less. But now?" He shook his head pityingly. "A scoundrel of the very worst kind." His little eyes examined Lyle, from the tall boots pulled high over his thighs to the crusty buff coat and long cloak that was the dark green of woodland moss. He scrutinised Lyle's face with its broad, clean-shaven chin and thin lips below a long, slightly canted nose. "I had hoped to run into you, Lyle, truth told. There are so many stories."

"All good, one hopes."

Walmsley spluttered derisively. "All ridiculous, judging by the measure I now have of you." He glanced quickly over his shoulder at his soberly presented companion. "The Major. Terror of the highways, scourge of the new regime." He hawked up a gobbet of phlegm, depositing it amongst the churned mud between Lyle's boots. "And yet here you are. A simple brigand."

Lyle cocked the pistol. "And yet I have you, sir." He let his gaze drift beyond the belligerent soldier. "And I have Sir Frederick Mason, do I not?"

The portly man in black seemed to colour at the mention of his name. "How...?"

"Lawyer by trade," Lyle went on. "I have been tracking you, sir. Waiting for you. You are my prey this night."

"Why?" Mason said, finally finding his voice.

"Because you are courtier to the new power in the land. Goffe's adviser and Cromwell's lapdog. A beneficiary of England's misery."

"He is the man," Walmsley cut in defiantly, "who'll drink a toast when he sees you dance from Tyburn Tree."

It startled everyone to hear the coach creak again and Lyle forgot the blustering soldier in an instant. He adjusted the pistol so that its muzzle was in line with the door, while he sensed the girl, still mounted to his right, bring her own pistol to bear.

"More of you?" he said to Walmsley, though he could hear the tension in his own voice. He imagined the coach might be more Trojan horse than gilt treasure.

Before Walmsley could respond, the head of a woman emerged from behind the curtain. Lyle simply stared. She was quite plainly clothed, in a dress of soft yellow, her auburn hair restrained about her scalp by a white coif. And yet Lyle found her utterly striking. It was the eyes, he knew. Dark and glittering, like nuggets of jet, the shape of almonds and the depth of oceans. They seemed to burn, boring right through him, reading his mind.

He swallowed thickly. "Your servant, mistress."

The woman stepped lightly out of the carriage. She was tall and slender, her lips full, scrunched together in a pout that he supposed was born of anger, though he found the gesture captivating. Sir Frederick, he realised, was speaking, and he shook his head, reluctantly tearing his gaze from this new vision. "By your leave, Freddy. I was too busy admiring your rather sumptuous friend."

The lawyer's cheeks filled with crimson. "Why, you devil-eyed villain. Insult a man's niece, would you?"

"Insult, sir? Far from it." He looked back at the woman. "I would but worship."

"How dare..." Sir Frederick began, but he was interrupted by the very woman he defended.

"It seems you know your captives, Major Lyle," she said. Her voice was surprisingly calm. "And we know you."

"Seems that way," Lyle agreed.

"Then why do your confederates cover their faces? Are they so hideous that they must not be beheld?"

That was a shrewd comment, thought Lyle, and he could not stifle a smile. "Adds to the mystique, mistress."

Her implacable expression did not falter. "Perhaps it masks their shame."

Lyle heard his companions chuckle at that and he could only laugh. "It is for their protection, mistress. For my part, I would have a jewel such as you gaze freely upon me."

"Haggard, is he not?" Grumm chirped from his place at the nervous horses, a bridle in each hand.

The woman appraised him. "You do not appear to take your vocation seriously, sir."

He knew she would be seeing a face more deeply lined than was befitting his twenty-six years, and eyes that, though a sparkling shade of green, had been described by former lovers as too cold to be truly attractive. Like the eyes of a hunting tomcat, one had said. He snatched off his wide-brimmed hat to reveal a mop of sweat-matted hair that was the colour of straw, and offered a short bow. "I have grieved too long to waste another moment on matters maudlin."

Her thin brows twitched a touch. "You chased our coach, sir. What kind of highwayman chases his quarry?" Her voice was hard, scornful, though he sensed a note of amusement too. "Would not a competent brigand have lain in wait? Blocked the road and so forth?"

Lyle cast a caustic glare at Grumm. "The element of surprise, mistress." He jerked the pistol, indicating that his prisoners should move to the side of the coach. "Now, if you would be so kind...."

They did as they were ordered, forming a line before Lyle. The girl dismounted too. "I'm Arabella," she announced in a friendly voice, though, as she ran a hand down the bristling Walmsley's flanks, her other still firmly gripped the pistol.

Lyle moved close to the woman. She seemed to stiffen under his gaze and he offered an impish grin. "I'll not check you for weapons, mistress, have no fear. I am a highwayman, not a lecher."

She made a display of sniffing the air. "I'd think you a gong farmer, sir, to tell by your aroma."

Lyle brayed at that. "You are a fine thing, and no mistake." He winked at her. "Might I have a name to put to the esteem?"

She seemed to be fighting back a smile, for the corners of her mouth twitched. "Felicity Mumford."

Lyle took up her hand and kissed it. "Angel."

"Unhand me, sir," Felicity protested, though she did not pull back.

"Push me away and I will be gone, by my honour."

Sir Frederick Mason was, Lyle knew, a political animal. One of the new men, risen by guile and wit in the aftermath of war. A grey-bearded snake. He was a wielder of quill and ink, rather than steel and shot, and, until now, his demeanour had reflected this fully. But the exchange with his niece seemed to invigorate the lawyer to action, for he stepped forward, jabbing a finger into Lyle's face. "Honour? Honour? You know nothing of the word!"

Lyle let Felicity's palm drop and stepped away. "This nation knows it not, Sir Freddy. No longer."

"Ah, here's the nub of it!" Mason squawked. "*Ironside* Highwayman. He dares use the name. This is no ironside. A *king's* dog, Felicity! Long gelded, but still he yaps!"

Lyle glanced across at Grumm. "Eustace, are the horses calmed?" He waited for a quick nod. "Then see to the loot."

"A pox on your thievery," Mason hissed. "God-rotten Cavalier."

"Innocent of that charge," Lyle replied, "I'm pleased to say."

"This man," Walmsley interceded, relishing his moment, "was once a hero of the rebellion. Would you countenance such a thing? A friend to Cromwell himself."

"Surely you jest, sir," the lawyer muttered, visibly thrown by the revelation. "Friend to the Protector?"

Lyle felt himself tense at the name. "Now his sworn enemy." He flashed a grin at Walmsley. "And always proud to school crusty old Roundheads in the ways of honour."

The soldier bridled, his blood up now, but it was his employer who spoke. "Cromwell is the best, godliest man in these islands. What depths do you plumb, sir, if you would make him your foe?"

"If those depths," Lyle replied levelly, "are to harangue, harry and plunder the men of Cromwell's new order, then they are waters in which it is a pleasure to swim." He let his eyes fall to the bulging flanks of Sir Frederick's heavy coat. "Now shall we peer into those deep pockets, sir?"

Walmsley stepped between them. "Stay where you are, Sir Frederick."

Lyle narrowed his eyes. "Steady, old man, lest you wish for some tutelage."

"Old man? I am Kit Walmsley. Formerly of Sir Hardress Waller's Regiment of Foot."

"Another of Oliver's toadies."

"Speak of the Lord Protector in such a manner..." Walmsley said through gritted teeth.

"Protector nothing, sir!" Lyle shot back scornfully. "That blackguard protects himself and nothing more. He ought to take the crown and abandon the obfuscation."

"Pup!" Walmsley blustered, his throat seeming to puff up like that of some red-faced bullfrog. "I'll cleave out your malignant tongue!" With that his hand was on his sword hilt, a third of the blade already exposed.

Lyle rolled his eyes. "Precious Blood! Must we?"

"Shoot 'im, Major," Eustace Grumm called impatiently. "Let's be on our way."

"You disgust me, Lyle," Walmsley went on, the rest of the sword sliding free. "You're a traitor and a coward and a quartering would be too lenient for you." His face warped into an expression of pure malice. "Perhaps we'll dig up your good wife and make her dead eyes watch."

Samson Lyle knew he was being goaded. He knew, most likely, that the sly Walmsley was playing for time. And yet the bastard had mentioned Alice.

He discarded his hat and tossed the pistol to Bella, who caught it with one hand, and released his own blade, its length slithering through the throat of his long scabbard. Taking half a dozen measured paces backwards, he held it out in front, dancing before Walmsley, the last light of the autumn eve dancing at its tip like molten silver. He felt good, powerful. He was tall, just touching six feet, with a body that was lean and spare, with muscles like braided match cord. A figure that betrayed a life of hardship, fight and flight. He cast a final glance at Grumm. "Take Star, Eustace. Turn him about."

Kit Walmsley stepped out, turning his shoulders to present the smallest possible target, right foot well advanced. "Turn him about? The horse cannot watch?"

"He cannot," Lyle said.

"Cannot witness his master take a beating?" the soldier asked incredulously. "Is the beast your mother, sir?"

"My companion through many horrors."

Sir Frederick called a subdued word of encouragement. Walmsley muttered something low and inaudible, his fleshy face suddenly taut with determination.

Lyle eyed him warily. A noise grumbled somewhere to his left, and he could not help but catch Grumm's sideways glance. He pretended to ignore the warning it contained, but acknowledged it inwardly all the same. For all Walmsley's advancing age, he retained the easy agility of a man much younger. Moreover, the way he drew his sword told of quick reflexes and a man not lacking in confidence. Indeed, the more Lyle saw of Walmsley, the more he thought the older man looked formidable: a leather-faced, compact, bullock of a man, exuding power and vigour.

Walmsley rumbled a challenge, waved him on. The highwayman stepped in. He was taller by a couple of inches, but a deal lighter. As the blade tips touched, tinkling musically, he felt the weight of his opponent push back, forcing him to brace himself as though standing before a great wave. He thought how it must have seemed to the onlookers like a fight between mastiff and whippet.

With a slash, Walmsley swept Lyle's blade aside, lunging straight in with an aggression that might have sent his steel all the way through the younger man's breast had not the whippet been wise to it. The highwayman jumped to his side, forcing himself to laugh contemptuously, though the hisses of his companions spoke of the closeness of the strike.

Walmsley thundered past like a wasp-stung boar, managed to keep his footing and wrenched his thick torso round to meet a counter from his enemy. None came, and he coughed up a wad of phlegm, deposited it at the roadside, and sneered. "What halts you, whelp? Your arrogance finally fades now that you face a real swordsman?"

The highwayman's blade was poised out in front, and he flicked his wrist so that the fine tip jerked. "Come."

They clashed, a flurry of clanging blows echoing from tree to tree like the song of mechanical birds.

"Were you at Worcester?" Walmsley asked as they parted again. "Or did you hide like the louse you have become?"

"I was," Lyle said. "And Naseby. And every other damnable place I was sent. My horse was with me, and it took its toll on him too, which is why he must face away for this. He dislikes fighting."

Walmsley shook his head in bewilderment, while Lyle could have sworn he heard Felicity Mumford laugh.

"I was at all the blood-soaked brabbles," Lyle went on, "fighting for the Parliament. And what was it all for? King Oliver the First!"

Walmsley's thick neck bulged as he grimaced, affronted by the insult, and he dipped his chin like an enraged stag, bolting forwards once more. The highwayman was again surprised by the bulky fighter's speed, and this time he had to offer a riposte before he could twist away. The weapons met high, crossed, blade sliding against blade in a teeth-aching hiss until hilts clanged.

Walmsley shoved forth, hoping to throw his opponent off balance, but Lyle gave ground willingly, letting the heavier man stumble in like a collapsing wall. They parted again, and this time Walmsley paused, heaving great, face-reddening gasps into labouring lungs. His eyes narrowed, the light of understanding glinting across their surface. He evidently sensed the younger man's game. Remain passive, cool and calm, venture no great attack, and offer no openings. Allow the bigger, older man to expend his energy, all the while defending, deflecting, moving clear.

"Blast you, sir, but you are a slippery knave," he rasped.

Lyle nodded. "And you a brave old curmudgeon. For that you have my utmost respect, sir, but I cannot allow you to carry this duel."

"Allow?"

Lyle looked across at Felicity Mumford and winked. "Observe."

Now he attacked, jabbing and cutting at Walmsley with speed. He saw each gap in the soldier's admittedly robust defences and took his chance, darting the razor tip of his sword through like a striking adder, forcing the rapidly tiring opponent to donate every ounce of strength in protecting his skin, all the while turning circles that would numb his legs as surely as if he ran all the way to London. Eventually, when he could see that Walmsley's face had taken on a purple hue at its edges, Lyle disengaged. "See that I battle with my elbow nicely bent?"

"What of it?" Walmsley blurted, bent double in an effort to coax air into his lungs.

"I use only my forearm to keep you at bay, while your hot forays drain you like a pistol-shot wine skin."

Walmsley grimaced. "Damn your impudence!"

"And my leading foot, you will observe, remains fixedly in front, ensuring my movements are made in a single line. Efficiency is key."

Walmsley attacked again, humiliation perhaps as invigorating as rage, but Lyle parried four ragged diagonal strikes, thrust his own blade along the lower line, as Besnard had taught him, and sent the soldier skittering rearward lest he lose a kneecap.

"You see, Kit," Lyle said, keeping his tone light, as though sharing some jolly anecdote with an old acquaintance. "May I call you Kit? One must fight to one's strengths. Paramount of which, for my part, are height, speed and stamina. The latter, particularly, will be nicely preserved whilst you hack and snarl your way to exhaustion." Lyle also reckoned upon his calmly delivered assessment, though entirely accurate, would serve to light a flame beneath the cauldron of Walmsley's rage, compelling him to lose all reason and bow only to furious temper.

The onslaught came as Lyle had expected. Walmsley drew himself to his full height, grasped the beautifully decorated hilt in both hands, and bolted forwards. A thunderous, snarling barrage of blows followed, each one propelled by white-hot fury and each carried on the crest of a wave given force by Walmsley's full weight. Lyle, for all his training, found himself compelled to retreat, for the jarring blows juddered up his fingers and wrist and arm, bludgeoning his shoulder like a cudgel. One of the old soldier's crushing downward thrusts bounced clear of Lyle's blade, only to sail perilously close to his right ear. It startled him into action, and he swayed out of range of the next backhanded swing and stepped smartly inside Walmsley's reach, thumping his hilt into the bullock-like opponent's face. The nose cracked noisily, Walmsley brayed, and blood jetted freely in a fine spray. Lyle came on, unwilling to afford his enemy time to recuperate, and Walmsley blocked his strike desperately, grunting with each move and staring through his new bloody mask with narrow, baleful eyes. A man, Lyle knew, with murder firmly on his mind.

Walmsley fell back suddenly in an effort to throw Lyle off balance, but the highwayman had anticipated the move and went with him, pricking the air before Walmsley's face in a series of staccato thrusts that had his eyes screwed tight as though a swarm of hornets buzzed about them. Walmsley, breathing hard now, gave more ground, slashing his blade in horizontal arcs as though swatting at the head of a leaping dog, all form vanished from his bearing. Lyle bore down swiftly upon him, so he twisted away, turning like a scarlet-cheeked acrobat, and lurched forth in a desperate lunge.

Lyle parried easily, twirled clear himself, and brought the blade down hard in a blow that would have split Walmsley's skull like a hammer against a boiled egg. The soldier blocked but had no riposte to offer, and Lyle let his sword slither along Walmsley's expensive steel, the rasp reverberating up his arm and through his ribcage. The guards met, Walmsley's ornate sword pressing hard against the functional bars of Lyle's weapon. There they stayed for a second or two, steel entwined like silver snakes, before Lyle darted back to break the zinging embrace. He allowed Walmsley to recover his feet. "Have you had enough, sir?"

"Never!" Walmsley snarled. He charged forth, slashing the sword wildly at the highwayman. Lyle parried the first mad blow, ducked below the second, stepped past Walmsley's thrashing body, and lashed the flat of his own blade against the soldier's rump. Walmsley howled, stumbled, and Lyle kicked him square in the back.

The fight had taken them near twenty yards away from the coach, and Samson Lyle paused to check that his captives were still where he had left them. Content, he advanced on his stricken foe. "Do you yield, sir?"

The fight had gone out of Kit Walmsley. He sat on his haunches, peering up at his conqueror, all defiance ebbed away. His round face was still bright with exhaustion, but no longer with rage, and his heavy jowls seemed to sag more than they had before. He tossed his sword away, ignominious defeat complete. "Where did you learn, sir?"

"To fight?" Lyle shrugged. "With the New Modelled Army."

Walmsley shook his head, beads of sweat showering his shoulders. "To fence."

Lyle thought back to the hours he had spent in the school of Charles Besnard, learning the great master's forms. The more he had absorbed, the less the memory of Alice had haunted him, and so he had worked day and night. "France. Rennes, to be exact. I did not enjoy exile, I admit, but it had its benefits."

He flicked Walmsley's sword into the air with his boot and caught it by the hilt, then turned away, leaving the broken man to trudge back to the coach nursing his shattered nose. "Eustace!"

Grumm, waiting patiently with Star and the two bays, looked up. "Major?"

"Is my most esteemed comrade well?"

Grumm patted the huge grey stallion on its dappled flank. "He's as irritable as ever, Major, aye."

"Good. Now, if you'd be so kind, please see what weighs so heavy in Lord Bed-Presser's pockets."

"Aye, Major." Grumm left the animals and moved quickly to where Sir Frederick Mason stood, his face a picture of indignation.

"Major?" Sir Frederick hissed, as Grumm took two purses from about the lawyer's person, both chinking with metal. "You're no officer, for you are no gentleman."

Grumm chortled. "I never yet seen a gen'lman made by his commission."

Lyle smiled. "Nor I."

He watched as Grumm moved swiftly to the rear of the coach and lifted a stout chest free. It was small, but clearly heavy, for Grumm groaned with the weight of it as he set it down. He turned when he sensed Walmsley at his back. "What is it?"

Walmsley glanced at the ornate blade still in Lyle's grip. "You'd leave a soldier without a sword, sir?"

"No, you're quite right, sir," Lyle agreed, slashing once through the air with the exquisite weapon, revelling in its astonishing balance. He drew his own sword and tossed it to Walmsley. "Enjoy," he said as he saw the rage come over the soldier again. "That piece of tin has bested many a great swordsman." He winked. "Including you." He looked abruptly away, not willing to enter into a discussion with the deflated soldier, and was pleased to discover the new blade fit snuggly into his scabbard.

Retrieving his pistol from Bella, he aimed it at the chest and fired. The crack of the gun echoed about the forest's darkening canopy, rooks and sparrows bursting up into the sky in fright, and the strongbox jumped back, its lid flung violently open in a spray of splinters. He turned to the prisoners even before the smoke had cleared, twisting the pistol's barrel and cocking it once more. "Two shots, remember." If Walmsley had intended to act, he evidently thought better of it, his gaze searching only his boots, and Lyle grinned broadly at Mason. "Now back in the carriage, Sir Freddy, and keep that blubbery jaw clamped or you shall see me upset."

Sir Frederick Mason hesitated, for he was incandescent with fury, yet he had seen the easy defeat of his experienced bodyguard and evidently preferred his skin to remain intact. With an almighty sigh, the lawyer waddled back to the vehicle and clambered awkwardly inside.

"Empty the box," Lyle ordered Bella, who immediately went to the damaged chest, a sack appearing in her hand.

He looked at the auburn haired woman who so captivated him. "Miss Mumford?"

Her eyes blazed with indignation. "You'll want my jewels, I suppose, you ruffian."

Lyle dropped his jaw as though scandalised. "Why, Felicity, we've only just met." She shot him a withering look, blowing a gust of air through her sharp nose, and he took her hand, guiding her to the coach door and helping her up the single step. He offered a quick bow. "It was a pleasure to make your acquaintance."

She turned back briefly, dark eyes searching his face. He thought he saw her lips lift in the merest hint of a smile. "I wish I could say the same."

***

Samson Lyle drew Star to a halt outside the barn. It was becoming dim now, and the old structure looked like a black rock amongst the trees, but he found its looming fastness reassuring, for they often used the abandoned place to regroup after a raid.

He slid nimbly off the side of the saddle, hitting the ground softly enough, though he felt his knee crack above the squelch of his boots. "Jesu, but I'm getting too old for this."

"Whereas," Grumm said as he reined in just behind, "I am still in fine fettle."

Lyle shot him a withering look. "Then next time, Eustace, you may wield powder and steel, while I shall hold the horses." There was a gnarled crab-apple tree nearby, its branches bare, clawing at the air like a crone's talons, and he tied Star to its trunk. He lingered for a short while to stroke the large patch of mottled pink skin that blighted the horse's handsome grey flank. The beast snorted irritably. "There there, boy," Lyle whispered, keeping his tone soft, soothing. "You did me proud as ever."

Grumm jumped down with an agility that belied his advancing years and brought his big black horse to the tree. "Rest up, Tyrannous."

Lyle sighed. "Must you call him that?"

"It means tyrant in the Greek," protested Grumm.

"I know what it means, Eustace," Lyle said as he checked the weapons held about Star's saddle. He had two pistols - the double-barrelled Dutch piece and a standard flintlock manufactured in London - along with the horseman's hammer he had carried through the civil wars.

He tugged on each, ensuring they were firmly in placc and always ready for deployment, and glanced up at the old man. "But it sounds ludicrous."

"What is ludicrous, Major," Grumm replied hotly, his neck sinews bulging, "is a highwayman with a cowardly and ever-vexed bloody horse!" He planted his hands on his hips. "You need a new mount."

"I need a new accomplice."

"I'm serious. His temper worsens by the month."

Lyle touched his fingertips to the grey's long face, tracing the white diamond that seemed to glow between its eyes in the darkness. Star pressed its muzzle into his palm and he glanced down at the damaged flank. "So would yours if you carried such a wound."

Grumm nodded. "If a cannon had exploded beside me, I'd be dead and gone, and I knows it. He's a strong bugger, no one's sayin' different. But you can't trust him." He tugged the strands of his straggly beard in exasperation. "It ain't right to have to avert the gaze of a destrier whenever there's a scrap."

"I trust him more than I trust you, old man," Lyle replied, thinking back to the ambush. "What happened back there?"

"As I already told you, Major, the branch we set was not long enough. It did not cover the road, and they went around."

"Leaving me to give chase. Christ, Eustace, it ain't good enough."

Grumm screwed up his face. "I'm a bloody smuggler, Major. I know weights and measures and the true value of goods. I know how to get things off the coast, where to keep 'em hid, and who to sell 'em to. We're all learning this new profession. All three of us together. Give us time."

Lyle snorted ruefully as they strode towards the large timber building. "Time? If they catch us we'll swing. No second chances, Eustace."

"Pah!" Grumm waved him away. "Quit your whining. Next time the branch'll be just perfect." He scratched at a globule of food that had dried fast amongst the tangles of his chin. "What did we get?"

Bella's mare, Newt, named for the jagged nature of her tail, was already tethered to an iron ring near the entrance to the barn, and the girl came striding out to greet them. She had long since discarded her scarf to reveal a face free of the blemishes of time. Her fresh, white skin only punctuated by a smattering of orange freckles across her nose and cheeks, and partially concealed by the shadow cast by a wide hat that she wore at a slant. "Some coin, a nice string of pearls, three gold rings, and that Walmsley's hanger."

Lyle nodded, drawing the sword he had taken from his bested opponent. "It is a Pappenheim."

Bella wrinkled her stubby nose, freckles briefly vanishing in the creases. "A pappy-who?"

"Pappenheim-hilt rapier. The style taken from Count Pappenheim, one of the imperial generals in the European wars." He held up the weapon, turning it slowly as though it were a rare gem. "Double edged and long enough to use from horseback. A gentleman's blade, but a murderer nevertheless." He ran a finger tenderly across the patterned hilt. "The guard is made of two distinct pieces. Not the full cup that one often sees, but a matching pair, like twin oyster shells, one set either side of the blade." Even the grey dusk failed to conceal the weapon's harsh beauty, and he could not help but marvel at the killing tool. Its pommel was ornately designed, heavy to offset the weight of the blade, but forged with some skill into the shape of a mushroom. The grip was tightly bound in good quality wire, and the sweeping knuckle bar twisted on its way from hilt to pommel, a subtle nod to the smith's craft.

"It is magnificent," Lyle said quietly. "But look here. The *pièce de résistance*." He fingered the holes that had been pierced into the two halves of the shell guard. "Stars and hearts. Perfectly formed," he turned the hilt over to examine the opposite half, "and perfectly symmetrical."

"Pretty," Bella said, lifting an eyebrow sardonically. She plucked off her hat, batting it with her other hand to send plumes of dust into the cool air.

"What was in that box?" Grumm asked impatiently.

"Hold your reins, Eustace," Lyle chided, smiling as he caught the glint of greed in the old smuggler's face.

Bella spat. "Paper."

"Paper?" Grumm echoed disbelievingly, his head wrenching hard round at the mercy of his tick.

Lyle raised a hand for quiet. "But what was written on it?"

She shrugged. "Piss-all, Samson."

He sighed. The girl had become his ward not long after Worcester, when Lyle still basked in the glory of revolution. The days when he had loved life, before things had turned sour between him and those for whom he had shed so much blood. She had been Dorothy Forks then. A snot-nosed urchin of six or seven, grubby-faced and barefooted. Lyle had been sent by his friend and master,

General Cromwell, down to Portsmouth to issue special orders to the garrison. Now, four years on, he could not remember the content of those orders, only the road along which he had travelled and the brief rest stop he had made. It was near a little hamlet in a winding part of the road that was thick with forest and birdsong. Star had dipped his muzzle into a tiny, moss-fringed stream, and Lyle had sat back on his rump and let the canopy-split sunlight dapple his face.

"Give us a groat, squire," the girl had said.

Lyle remembered his eyes snapping open to gaze up at the feral face with its twinkling hazel eyes. "Give?" he had asked, amused by her precociousness. "You do not work for your keep?"

"Oh, I work, squire. Work 'ard." She had been wearing a baggy shirt that was almost the colour of the soil at their feet, and she wriggled her bony shoulders once, twice, and the garment was bunched at her waist. "Work on you, if it please ya."

Lyle had been astonished and repelled at once. "On me? Christ, girl, but you're a child."

She had winked in a perverse attempt at appearing coquettish. "One what can polish your privy member till it gleams."

Lyle had found himself on his feet, as though the very notion had put him on edge. "You do this often?"

"Aye, sir, as oft as I must."

"Must? Who puts you to such a task? What manner of man?"

The man in question had appeared then, stalking round the bend in the road with a face ravaged by pox and sharpened by greed. He had grinned obsequiously upon eyeing the exchange, bowed low over his gnarled cane, and explained in more detail the services his girl could offer a fine gentleman with coin and discretion. Lyle had snapped the cane across its owner's skull, leaving him senseless in the long grass, and gathered little Dorothy up into his saddle. They had not parted since. He had insisted she learn her letters, and she had insisted he never address her by her old name again.

Bella had travelled Europe with him in the intervening years, learning skills with weapons as well as books, yet she still wielded the brazen tongue that had so intrigued him at that first meeting. He watched as she went to fetch the sack into which the chest's contents had been thrust. "Piss-all to your eyes, maybe, but what exactly do they say?"

She grimaced as she took out a handful of sheets. "It's just a bunch o' letters, Samson."

Lyle held out a hand. "Let me see."

"Shouldn't bother," Eustace Grumm muttered as he went to urinate against the barn. "It's too damned dark. You'll bugger your eyes."

"Aye, I suppose," Lyle relented. "Back at the Lion then. We'll study them by candlelight."

"Don't know why we didn't just ride there direct," Grumm said as he hoisted up his breeches. "Ale's what a man needs after a take. Gives him a thirst."

"Gives a woman a thirst too," Bella agreed, nodding enthusiastically. "And we've some pigeon pie left over."

Grumm grimaced, his tick rampant. "Mightn't be the case, young Bella."

"You greedy old beggar," the girl said, an accusatory finger stabbed in Grumm's direction.

"As I've told you before," Lyle cut in quickly, "we do not make for home immediately after a take. If we're tracked, then let them track us here."

He felt a tremor then. It took a few moments for the sensation to filter up through his boots, but the feeling was so familiar that he knew instantly what it was. The others were staring at him. They had both come a long way since joining him in this new perilous adventure, but neither had stood on a battlefield and let the earth's vibrations whisper to them. Neither had that perception of danger that only experience could give. "To your mounts," he heard himself say.

"Major?" Grumm asked, his bearded face suddenly tense.

Bella stepped forward a pace. "Samson, what is it?"

"To your mounts, damn you!" Lyle snapped suddenly, spinning on his heels to make for the crab-apple tree where Star grazed. "We are hunted!"

Bella and Grumm rode clear of the barn as soon as the horsemen were in sight. It was an oft practised ploy, for Lyle's pursuers seemed to grow in number and tenacity with every robbery he committed, and the only way the three of them could hope to even the odds was by splitting the hunting party. Thus the girl and the smuggler would ride in opposite directions, while Lyle would take a third route, and they would trust their skins to the speed of their mounts and the encroaching darkness, hoping to meet much later at the rendezvous point.

Lyle cursed his nonchalance as he clambered into the saddle. Felicity Mumford had mocked him for playing at criminal as though it were a game, and, he inwardly admitted, it was a sharper thrust than she knew. He had become good at his new profession, and that had made him blasé, while his fury at the world had made him reckless. He had always insisted that Bella and Grumm conceal their faces during an ambush, telling himself that it would keep them safe, but deep down he knew that his own behaviour would eventually negate any such safeguard. Why had they spent so long at the barn? Why had he chosen to inspect his loot before they were safely back home? No reason, he chided himself as Star gathered pace to a brisk canter, beyond pure arrogance. He prayed they would make good their escape.

Star burst through a stand of withered brown bracken and out onto the moonlit road. Lyle stood in his stirrups to squint at the approaching posse. There were six of them, and he knew their presence was unlikely to be mere coincidence, for they each wore scarfs the colour of saffron about their torsos and waists, the device carried by many of the men who served William Goffe, the new Major-General of Berkshire, Sussex and Hampshire. Such men were no longer simply the army - they were the law - and to see them riding in strength about a night-fallen backwater spoke of a purpose beyond routine. Orders were bellowed from the lead rider and the main group seemed suddenly to dwindle, the rearmost of their number peeling skilfully away. Good, Lyle thought. Divide and conquer. He raked his spurs viciously along Star's flanks and the big stallion roared its anger, reared briefly, and sped away. He twisted in the saddle to see how many of the pack remained. To his surprise, there was only one, and, though the distance was too great to make out the man's features, he could see enough of the rider to identify him. He was clad in the ubiquitous hide and metal of a cavalry trooper, his head encased in a helmet with a single sliding nasal bar and a tail of riveted steel sheets to protect his neck. In all this, the horseman might have been any nameless trooper thundering along this rain-softened bridleway, but for his scarf. Swathing his torso diagonally, fastened in a large knot at his side like a vast flower in bloom, the garment was made unique by a black smudge at the point where the voluminous material crossed its wearer's shoulder. Lyle could not see the detail, but he knew the device well enough, and the revelation gave him pause. He hauled on Star's reins, stooped forth to whisper into the skittish stallion's pricked ear. "I won't run from him."

Lyle instructed the snorting beast to turn with deft movements of his wrists and thighs, and Star did as he was bidden, hooves sliding alarmingly in the mud. But he was steady enough, and soon they faced their pursuer, moving into a lively trot.

The man in the orange scarf was at a gallop now, and his big black horse devoured the ground in a matter of moments. Lyle saw him draw a pistol and he produced the short English flintlock holstered to his left. He was reticent to fire, for Star hated the sound, and the report would doubtless tempt the rest of the posse back to his position, but the armoured man discharged his weapon immediately, its sharp cough making Lyle shrink low behind his steed's thick neck. Star bellowed like a bullock at Smithfield and it was all Lyle could do to keep control, but eventually he was able to straighten and take aim. He shot when the rider was still thirty paces away, knew he had missed, and dropped the reins so that he might draw his second firearm. His attacker had another pistol too, and it was fired quickly, the report agonisingly loud now that they were so close. Lyle ducked, even as his hand groped madly for the butt of his double-barrelled gun, but the lead flew over his right shoulder to smack into a tree some distance behind. Now he had the advantage, levelled his pistol, but the trooper raced past before he could cock the hammer, slashing at Lyle with a hefty looking broadsword, and the highwayman only just managed to avoid its murderous arc, the pistol skipping from his grip to tumble into a muddy rut.

The foes wheeled about to face one another again. Lyle felt Star's huge bulk judder beneath him, and he knew the battle-scarred animal was beginning to panic. He had to forgo his blade so that he might cling on with both hands, desperate to keep himself in the saddle, even as the saffron-scarfed pursuer bore down again. He knew he would be skewered this time and, just as the horses were about to meet, he wrenched savagely on Star's reins, tearing the bit to compel the steaming grey away from the line of collision. Star slewed violently to the right, Lyle felt himself sway in the saddle, his rump sliding precariously out of position, and his thighs screamed in pain as he clamped them tight. Somehow he stayed on, the trooper's blade cleaving nothing but crisp air, and then he was into the trees, pounding along a narrow track that was fringed with tangled branches and perilously dark. He could not hear a thing above Star's thrashing breaths, but he twisted back to see that the armoured man had given chase, despite the risk to his own mount. Lyle leaned in to whisper encouragement in the horse's ears, and was immediately gratified to sense a calming in the frightened animal's demeanour.

"There you are, Star, old thing," he said, slapping the stallion's hard neck. "Keep your nerve and we'll see what can be done."

The trees thinned and the track widened until Lyle found himself in a small grove. It was skirted by ancient looking boughs, the kind Grumm often talked of when telling tales of the first people of his native Cornwall, and strangely illuminated by the moon. He let Star run across it but wheeled him around as soon as they reached the far side.

The man on the black mount burst out from the woods to meet them and drew his horse to a halt. "I have you now, Lyle!"

Lyle felt exhausted from the chase, but he forced himself to doff his hat in mock salute. "Well bless me, if it isn't the Mad Ox of Hampshire!"

The trooper's face was bisected by the nasal bar and obscured in the horse's billowing breaths, but Lyle caught the flash of white teeth below a bushy black moustache as he sneered. "Have a care, sir, for the life of a brigand seldom ends well."

"Soldier, Francis!" Lyle called back. "Not brigand."

"You are outside the law!"

Lyle laughed. "Because the law in this county is but one man; William Goffe. And you, Francis, are Goffe's creature."

The trooper bristled, kicked forwards a touch, sword still naked and glinting. The black motif embroidered at his shoulder now resolving into the gaping maw of a roaring lion. "It is Colonel Maddocks to you, Lyle."

Lyle drew his own sword now that he was confident that Star had found some semblance of calm. "And it is Major Lyle to you."

Maddocks urged his mount to the right so that it walked the perimeter of the clearing. "You relieved Sir Frederick Mason of some valuables this night. I want them back."

"Not possible," Lyle countered. A thought occurred to him. "You clung to my tail with impressive haste, Colonel. Too soon for Sir Freddy to have reported our encounter. Were you supposed to have been his escort?"

"I'm warning you, Lyle," Maddocks snarled. "Return the items forthwith."

Lyle laughed. "I'm right! You should have been protecting him. Stone me, sir, but such a thing will not go well for your prospects, eh? But why would they appoint you personally? The Major-General's private mastiff sent on an errand such as this. A tad beneath you, is it not?"

"How long do you think you can last?" Maddocks called suddenly. "Out here on the road."

"Long enough," Lyle called back, moving Star to mirror his opponent so that they circled one another like a pair of ban-dogs in a Southwark pit.

"Goffe has made me your nemesis, Lyle. I am his chief huntsman now. The snare closes around you, never doubt it."

"And yet I will ever wriggle free."

"To what end?"

He had often wondered upon that question. The war was over. The old king dead and gone, his son hiding away in France. The bastions of the Royalist cause; Prince Rupert, Lucas, Montrose, were scattered to the wind, or rotting in mocked graves. The Scots cowered to the north and Ireland was subjugated. It was what Lyle had prayed and worked towards his whole life. Complete victory. And yet, the sweet taste of a true republic had quickly soured. "There is no end as long as tyrants stalk the land. We fought and died to throw off the yoke of one, and were straight-way given another. Goffe is no better than Laud or Strafford."

Maddocks spat. "Major-General Goffe is invested with the Lord Protector's authority. He is a righteous man. Anointed by..."

"By God?" Lyle shouted across the grove. "Do you not hear yourself, Maddocks? The Divine Right of Major-Generals!" He shook his head in disbelief. "What did we fight for all those years? You and I, side by side, taking back these isles inch by bloody inch, and for what? A king in all but crown. A nation carved up and served in slices for Cromwell's friends to feast upon. A land ruled on the private whims of generals."

Maddocks seemed to be grinning behind the iron bar. He levelled the sword, pointing it like a steel finger at the outlaw. "You were Cromwell's man once, Lyle. Do not play false with me. You were content enough with your lot until it no longer sat pretty with your feeble sensibilities."

The image of the colonel across the grove seemed to dim then, as though his darkening silhouette became part of the elm-thrown shadows, and other shapes slithered over Lyle's mind. Other men, womenfolk and children, running, screaming, weeping. They were shrouded in a mist that was red as an April dusk, a shade ever branded upon his memory; blood and fire.

Ireland. That was where it had all started. He had been there for some months, serving Ireton, mopping up the last remnants of resistance at Carlow, Waterford and Duncannon as the New Modelled Army rolled over the land like an inexorable storm cloud. The battles had been hard fought and well won, and he had thanked God daily for His providence. And then came the massacres. There had been plenty of blood spilt already, for the Confederate War had raged since before even the English struggles, but Lyle had not borne witness to it, and he had learnt quickly that tall tales were the currency of soldiers and civilians alike. Yet at Limerick his eyes had been prized open like clams in a cauldron. He had seen things - done things - that even now he could not begin to reflect upon, lest bile bubble to his throat. So many innocents had died, all for a greater good that he increasingly found impossible to espouse. What still astonished him was his own arrogance. The conceited nature of a young, brash, infamous soldier that told him to confront his commander as if his voice could possibly be heeded. He had considered himself friend to Henry Ireton, a brother-in-arms, and that had convinced him to speak his mind. How foolish he had been.

Maddocks attacked. He spurred forth with a sudden kick that had his horse bellowing and his opponent reeling. It was all Lyle could do to urge Star into a run, and he managed to raise his blade in the nick of time as the pair met in the open ground, suddenly close enough to see the whites in each other's eyes. The weapons met high with a clang, pressed in, flashing in the moonlight as they filled the deep forest with the song of swords. Lyle looked into Maddocks' face to see his old comrade's rictus grin, lips peeled back in a grimace made all the more horrifying by the black eyes that were screwed narrow with determination. Lyle twisted the blade to free the deadly embrace, felt the tip of the colonel's sword bounce off one of the shell guards protecting his hand, and was immediately thankful to have obtained such a weapon, even as he was forced to parry two more strikes from the formidable opponent. He managed to sway back to avoid the third short thrust and steered Star out of range.

"You are a mad cur, Lyle," Maddocks rasped as the horses wheeled about. "Foolish, blinkered and vain."

"Better a free fool than chained."

"Chained? That horse bolted a long time ago." Maddocks swiped the air with his heavy sword. "It'll be the noose or nothing for you."

Lyle laughed. "Then I choose nothing."

"The choice is not yours to make."

The colonel came again, bolting impressively forwards from a standing start, but this time Lyle was ready for him. He squeezed his thighs lightly, flicked the reins, and Star slewed away, leaving Maddocks' mount to charge into the cool air in his wake. He turned, even as Maddocks rallied for another assault, slicing his own arc above Star's tall ears in an ostentatious blur. "You may chase me, Mad Ox, but you will not take me alive! I'll fight Goffe's creatures as long as I draw breath!"

"The war is over, Lyle," Maddocks countered.

Lyle shook his head as he rolled his shoulders for the next engagement. "Not for me."

"It was Ireton killed her, Samson," said Maddocks, his tone softening a touch. "His orders. Not Goffe, not Cromwell."

"But Ireton is dead."

"Then the debt dies with him."

Lyle dipped his head as he kicked. "No."

They raced inward, closing the ground in a heartbeat, but this time Lyle released the reins, gripping with legs only, and unhooked the iron war hammer that hung beside his shin. It was two-thirds of a yard in length, the four-sided hammer counterbalanced by a lethally sharp pick, and he hurled it at Maddocks' horse. The big beast cried out as the heavy club slammed into its shoulder, and it lost its step enough to put Maddocks off his swing. The colonel's broadsword found nothing but clean air, and Lyle brought his own blade round to clatter the side of the soldier's head. Maddocks' helmet saved his life, but the force of the blow knocked him sideways so that he slid halfway off the saddle. The disquieted horse, still whinnying in pain, reared up, throwing him clear so that he finished in a heap of leather and metal in the centre of the grove.

Lyle was upon him in moments, snatching up the war hammer as he moved to stand over his stricken enemy. He held it up as Maddocks stared forlornly back, wincing with each breath. "An outdated old thing, really. Made for smashing plate armour. Has its uses, though, I'm sure you'll agree."

Maddocks spat a globule of blood that looked like tar in the night. "Get it over with."

"When they killed her," Lyle said, "were you there?"

Maddocks seemed surprised at the question, but he managed to shake his head. "I was not."

"I never saw her body. Never had the chance to kiss her cold lips or put her in the ground myself."

"Alice had a good burial, Samson," Maddocks said. "But you were on the run. A deserter."

Lyle nodded. "It was my fault, I know. And the knowledge that I was not at home when the soldiers came has eaten me alive these four years. I was not there to protect her, as was my duty." He forced a smile that seemed so at odds with his feelings. "But that knowledge has driven me too. Given me purpose that had all but leaked away in Ireland."

"Just kill me now, damn you!" Maddocks snarled suddenly, the wait for his demise crushing his spirit as he gazed up at the stars.

"I will not," Lyle said. He went to gather up Star's reins and clambered nimbly into the saddle, putting the weapons away and offering a sharp bow. "You are bested, Francis, and I will best you again, and again, for as long as you hunt me. The war is not yet done. It is a war of vengeance, against those who wronged me, chased me away from my home and murdered my wife. A war against the Protector's creatures. It will never be done."

***

The Red Lion was a modest establishment just off the Portsmouth to London Road at a village called Rake. It had stabling for half a dozen horses, lodgings enough for the same number of travellers, and a decent sized taproom stocked with good local ale and a passable claret. It was also the perfect place from which a highwayman might launch his campaign.

"What happened?" Eustace Grumm's voice came from the darkness as Lyle dismounted in the small courtyard outside the inn.

Lyle peered into the gloom. He could see the reed-thin profile of his friend leaning casually against the red brick wall, soft candlelight streaming through the windows to highlight him a touch. "It was Maddocks."

Grumm had a clay pipe clamped between his crooked teeth and he pulled it free, blowing a large pall of smoke as he spoke. "In the flesh?"

"Aye."

"Knew it were Goffe's men by the scarves, but I hadn't expected the Mad Ox to ride with them. You're sure?"

"I knew from a long way off," Lyle nodded, whistling softly for the stable hand to collect Star. "Saw his crest."

"The black lion?"

Lyle tapped his shoulder. "Embroidered into his scarf, here."

Grumm snorted. "Very nice. Must be doin' well for himself these days."

Lyle nodded. "He is tasked with hunting me down, it seems. Major-General Goffe's right-hand."

Grumm stepped out of the shadows, his eyes like white orbs in the night. "You spoke?"

"We fought."

Grumm's jaw dropped, but footsteps scraped on the yard's compacted chalk and both men turned to see a young girl appear from the stables. "Take yer 'orse, m'lord?" Bella asked with a mischievous grin.

Lyle smiled as he handed her the reins. Her role in charge of the stables was a source of great pride, but many of her customers were also victims out on the road, and the irony was not lost on her. "I am glad you made it."

She grinned. "Never in doubt. Those old buggers in armour never outrun me an' Newt." Her freckled nose wrinkled as she inspected Lyle's saddle, and she reached up to draw the double-barrelled pistol. "You didn't have the same luck though, I'm guessin'."

Lyle took the weapon from her and turned it in his hand. The piece was caked in half-dry mud, from muzzle to butt, and would need a thorough clean before it would function. "Dropped on the road. I was lucky to retrieve it."

"Dropped?" Bella echoed incredulously.

"Christ above!" Grumm blurted as he squinted at the filthy weapon. "I knows why you bloody dropped it." He thrust a spindly finger in Star's direction. "That nag'll be the death of you, Major."

Lyle followed the former smuggler's gaze. "Will you sing that same tired tune all your life, Eustace?"

"I'll sing it every time he near kills you, aye!"

"There was a moment," Lyle confessed, "after Maddocks and I exchanged fire, that I almost lost control. He panicked, looked to bolt. I could feel it."

Grumm fiddled with his straggly beard. "Damn me, Major. If you're not fighting the toughest bugger in Goffe's retinue, you're wrestling with your own mount."

Bella patted the horse. "Ah, don't mind him, Star." She glared at Grumm. "He's a sour old thing."

The old man jammed his pipe stem back between his teeth. "Not so sour as that bloody animal."

Lyle went to the horse, scratching the white diamond between its big eyes and receiving a soft nudge of its snout for his trouble. "He may be shy on occasion, but did you ever see a swifter beast? He's saved my skin more than times than I could count. I'll not turn my back on him now. Besides," he added, speaking into the animal's twitching ear, "we won, didn't we, boy?"

"Good work, Samson," Bella declared happily. "The Mad Ox is a proper fighter."

"When we rode together with the ironsides," Lyle said, tucking the pistol into his waistband, "he was one of the very best. Better than me, that's for certain."

"What's changed?" Eustace Grumm asked.

"All that fencin', I bet," said Bella. "Them hours an' hours with that glum-guts Besnard."

Lyle could not help but laugh at that. "Actually, I threw my hammer at his horse. Now come along. I need ale."

The three of them sat at the taproom's rearmost table, lit by fat beeswax candles and wreathed in smoke from Grumm's pipe. There was one other patron, slumped in a far corner cradling a pot of strong beer, but they recognised him from the village and knew he posed no threat. Grumm had fetched victuals while Bella had seen to the horses. There were some hard-edged offerings from the cheese cratch, thin strips of bacon, and good bread, cooked in the ovens on the premises, and the trio were soon enjoying a well-earned meal. If the bell jangled at the door, they would shift into well practised action. Lyle would be gone, vanished into the shadows and out through the small rear door that would take him to the woods beyond, while the others would inhabit their roles of tapster and stable-hand like a pair of players in the long-defunct theatres that had hugged the southern bank of the Thames. Eustace Grumm ran the tavern, going by the name of John Brown, while Bella was his great-niece, Lucy. It had worked for a year, ever since Lyle had returned from France with his two rather incongruous companions and a tidy fortune made at the sharp end of a duellist's blade. The charade had given them a business, a place of relative safety from the wolves of the road, and it had become the home none of them had thought ever to find. A secure bolthole away from their life of crime, and yet all the while funded by it.

Lyle took out his prized pistol and placed it on the table. He began to pick at the flaky mud with his fingernails, scraping away the road's grime to reveal the magnificent weapon beneath. When the larger lumps were scoured clear, he took up a cloth and worked at the more intricate parts of the lock.

"You threw your war-hammer at him," Grumm muttered in amusement, bits of half-chewed bread flecking his beard as he spoke. "What would Master Besnard think?"

"He would congratulate me on staying alive. And he'd tell you not to stare down that beak of yours so sanctimoniously."

Grumm crammed a chunk of cheese into the side of his mouth. "He'd advise you to pick your fights more carefully."

Lyle looked up from the pistol. "I won, didn't I?"

"Barely."

As she worked her way through a plate of bacon that was scorched crisp, Bella leafed through the pile of papers she had taken from Sir Frederick Mason's strongbox. She glanced at Lyle, her expression sour. "Like I said, Samson. Piss-all in this lot."

Lyle gnawed a grubby fingernail. "Keep looking. Sir Frederick must have been carrying something of significance for Maddocks to be shadowing him."

"Fat lot o' good he did," Grumm said happily.

"Yet the fact remains," Lyle said. "He had Walmsley in the carriage for close protection, but Maddocks was already out on the road. He tracked us so quickly, he can't have been far behind Mason."

"Lucky we jumped him when we did," Bella said.

Grumm cackled. "They was to rendezvous before they hit the Combe, I'd wager."

"You may be right," said Lyle, for it seemed reasonable. Between the villages of Hill Brow and Rake, the London Road climbed above a deep, wooded vale known as Harting Combe. In the summer months, when the going was firm, travellers could gaze down upon the Combe as they thundered along, enjoying the clean air and the stunning view. But the road south of Rake was very steep as it plunged off the high ground, becoming almost impassable during autumn and winter when the terrain was water-logged and filthy. Those on foot might still risk the shorter route, or even skilled riders if they possessed a good mount, but no heavy vehicle could begin to negotiate so sharp a gradient in such precarious conditions. They would be forced, then, to risk the low, forest-choked bridleway that curved along the foot of Harting Combe, meeting the main highway again at a point beyond London Road's steep drop. It avoided that difficult section of road, which was a blessing, but it forced pilgrims to take their chances in the dense woodland of the isolated vale, compelling those travellers of a wealthier nature to ensure they were well protected. Mason, Lyle had guessed, would be one such person, and he had decided to strike the lawyer at the Combe's southern edge, for many a coach had met with an armed escort before taking the road down into the forest's infamous embrace. Evidently it had been a good gamble to make, for Colonel Maddocks and his troopers were almost certainly due to link up with Mason at Hill Brow. They had intercepted their quarry in the nick of time. He gnawed his lip as he considered the implication. "Why Maddocks?"

"That Mason's one o' Goffe's big wheels," Bella answered. "You said so yourself."

"But so is Maddocks." He shook his head. "Why set his best man to protecting a lawyer? No, it was not Mason himself that was significant. Rather what he was carrying. We must reflect upon our takings."

Bella shrugged. "Not much. Just a few trinkets."

"Which means," Lyle persisted, "it was the strongbox."

The girl sighed theatrically as she delved into the scraps of paper again. "How many bushels o' corn they got in store. A letter from the Major-General askin' Mason to settle a dispute 'tween farmers down at Rowlands Castle." She waved one crumpled sheet. "Message informing Sir Blubber-Belly that a prisoner's to be moved from Newbury to Portsmouth."

"What prisoner?" Lyle asked.

She shrugged. "Don't say." She looked through the papers again, pausing at one. "Now this'n is an invitation from Sir John Hippisley for Mason to attend a masquerade, whatever that is."

"A masquerade ball," Lyle explained. "A grand dance. Very popular in France. The people will wear disguises."

"Surprised Goffe would allow such a decadent thing," Grumm grunted. "Smacks of Cavalier to me."

"He probably doesn't know," replied Lyle. "Hippisley's out at Hinton Ampner, is he not? On the Winchester Road."

Bella scanned the paper and nodded. "The manor house, aye."

Grumm looked up with a mocking sneer, a trail of fat wending its way down his beard from the corner of his thin mouth. "Surprised you don't attend, Major, given your apparent lust for death." He shook his head in exasperation. "Congratulate you for staying alive, would he? Besnard would have you whipped through the streets for such recklessness."

That was true, thought Lyle. When he had enlisted with Besnard after a couple of months of listless wandering, he had been an angry, desperate, grief-stricken youth. He had sold his armour to buy food, leaving only the grimy clothes on his back, a big, wounded horse, and his much dented sword. Charles Besnard had seen him fight an ill-judged duel over an unpaid debt - one he had been lucky to survive - and had seen some spark of promise in the way Lyle had handled his blade. He had taken the Englishman on, given him and Bella lodgings, and taught him the ways of the great fencing masters. Besnard had saved Lyle, without a doubt, but he could still be a strict disciplinarian who would not have entertained or condoned the rekindling of Lyle's thirst for danger. "Come now, Eustace," he said calmly, "you know more than most about staying alive. For a righteous man, you've done your fair share of unrighteous acts in the name of saving your skin."

Grumm sat back and took a drag on his pipe. "We are not discussing me, Major."

"How many ships did your false light guide onto Clovelly rocks so that you might eat?"

That hit a nerve, for the old man lurched forwards to jab the clay stem at Lyle's face. "I was never a wrecker, damn your forked tongue!"

Lyle smiled, holding up placating palms. "A smuggler then."

"Aye, a smuggler," Grumm conceded, aware that Lyle was goading him and at pains to cool his ire, "and proud to say it. But a wrecker never. If you were any other man, Major Lyle, I'd stick my boot in your behind for such slander."

"Easy, Eustace, easy. My point is that we play the hand life deals us, and do what we must to survive."

Grumm eased back again, half disappearing in the billowing smoke. "Amen to that."

"And next time I shall open Maddocks from chest to ballock."

Grumm chuckled. "No you won't. You enjoy the chase as much as he."

Lyle offered a shrug, for he could not argue with so observant a man. He held up the pistol instead. "Look at her. Such beauty." It had been made by a gunsmith in Rotterdam, though Lyle had picked it up after a tavern brawl on the outskirts of Rennes not long after his flight from England. It had been there that he had bade his time after his world had collapsed, and there that he had learnt a modicum of French and a great deal of swordsmanship. He lifted the pistol with both hands, for, though barely heavier than a typical English flintlock, it was longer by the length of his hand, from wrist to fingertips. He blew gently over the lock to make sure no loose powder or debris from the ride had lingered amongst the mechanism. Satisfied, he checked the strikers. There were two, which was what made this weapon so special - and so lethal. Double-barrelled handguns were rare enough, but one with only one lock was almost unheard of. This pistol had two barrels, one set above the other. When Lyle fired the piece, he need only depress the barrel release, twist the twin muzzles round, and fire again. The same lock, cock and flint would be employed, making the process swift and simple.

Grumm stared at it. "Just don't drop the damned thing next time, Major. She's your talisman. That extra shot will save your life one day."

The sound of Bella chuckling excitedly made both men look down at her. She had a heavily creased square of vellum in her pale hand, which she thrust under Lyle's nose. "Finally the cull cackles!"

"What is it?" Lyle asked.

"That prisoner, Samson. Goes by the name of James Wren."

"Sir James Wren was a lieutenant-colonel of harquebusiers. Rivalled Prince Robber in the saddle. I fought him once."

It was late. The last patron had staggered out into the crisp night air, and the Red Lion's heavy studded door had been locked and barred. The candles guttered, throwing eerie shapes on the whitewashed walls, while the last remnants of flame danced in the hearth. Bella had cleared away the detritus of the meal, replacing their ale with steaming pots of spiced wine, and now the three outlaws sat together at the age-scarred elm table, a strangely concocted family who knew that each night together could be their last.

"Fought *with* him?" Eustace Grumm asked, staring at Lyle over the rim of his wooden pot.

"Fought him," Lyle repeated. "A skirmish in the days before Worcester." He took a swig of wine as he remembered those frantic times when the son of the deposed king had returned to lay claim to the crown. The young king had been smashed by Cromwell's far superior New Modelled Army, a battle that had effectively put an end to the wars that had stolen a decade from the people of the British Isles. Cromwell had called Worcester a *crowning mercy*, but all Lyle remembered was bloodshed and panic, and a populace worn to wraiths by plague, starvation and fear. "Lucky to get out of it with my hide in one piece."

"A king's man?" said Grumm.

"None more so."

Grumm raised his pot. "May he rot, then." He took a long draught, belching when he was done, and wiped his glistening beard with a grubby sleeve. His eyes narrowed as they searched Lyle's face. "And yet?"

"And yet it would seem he now languishes in Goffe's clink," Lyle replied. "If he's to be moved down to Portsmouth, then perhaps transportation awaits."

"Why would you care? An old enemy imprisoned by a new one."

Lyle shrugged. "Because the enemy of my enemy is my friend, Eustace. Wren was an honourable fellow, for all his malignant allegiance, and I would see him free if it hurt the Protectorate."

Grumm still stared hard at his friend, his blue eyes alive with suspicion. "I do not like that look."

"You mentioned a masquerade?" Lyle said, snapping his head round to address Bella. "Hippisley's place at Hinton Ampner?"

"Aye," Bella nodded. She clutched her pot in both hands, cradling the warm vessel against her chest as though it were full of precious gems.

Lyle drank slowly, luxuriating in the spices that fought away the autumn eve. "Not far from here. Out to the west above the Winchester road. When was this event to take place?"

"On the morrow," replied the girl. She gathered up a handful of the long, mousy hair that fell to her shoulders, running it through her fingers, her face wistful. "Wish I could be a great lady at a dance."

Lyle grinned. "You are already a great lady. But perhaps your wish is not so far-fetched. I believe we have our solution, praise God."

"Our solution?" Grumm spluttered as Bella beamed. "You cannot possibly..."

"Worry not, old fellow," Lyle cut in. "You need not embroil yourself in this."

Grumm lifted his pot. "Suits me well, and no mistake." When he had swallowed, he fixed the highwayman with a drilling stare. "You're a damnable fool, Samson Lyle, I do not mind telling you."

Lyle raised a single eyebrow. "Evidently."

"Anyone who is anyone will be there, for Christ's sake. God-rotten magistrates. Bureaucrats. Soldiers. Any number of Major-General Goffe's lackeys." He shook his head in bewilderment. "Zounds, the Mad Ox too, I shouldn't wonder." He leaned in suddenly. "He knows what you bloody look like, you fool!"

"But not what *you* look like," Lyle replied. "Or Bella. Besides, it is a masquerade. Every man and woman will wear a disguise." He rubbed thick fingers over the emerging bristles of his chin, the scraping sounds seeming unnaturally loud in the empty taproom. "I have to go, Eustace. I have to go. If Sir Frederick Mason is in attendance then we may discover when they plan to move Wren. It is a chance to strike at our enemies."

"Well do not count on my assistance, you bee-headed bloody frantic," Grumm retorted hotly. He folded his arms, setting his jaw and staring at the blackened beams above. "I shan't have any part in it, as God is my witness."

PART TWO: THE DANCE

Hinton Ampner, Hampshire, November 1655

Hinton Ampner was a tiny village straddling the road between Petersfield and Winchester. The land was thick with forests that stretched in all directions into the chalky South Downs, only occasionally broken up by patches of open farmland that sustained the smattering of timber-framed hovels clustered like toadstools about the hamlet's core. And that core was the Manor House, the huge edifice of red brick and grey stone that had been built in Tudor times as a hunting lodge and grown into the most imposing structure for miles.

It was evening as Samson Lyle and Eustace Grumm stepped over the threshold. The surrounding trees darkened an already grey dusk, but the great house glowed bright, basking in the tremulous light of a thousand candles. No stinking tallow, Lyle noted, for Sir John Hippisley had done well out of the revolution, seen his star rise with the other hard men of the new order, and the old Roundhead's home was sweet with the scent of beeswax, a touch of wood smoke and a great deal of perfume.

A footman in a fine suit of shimmering red and blue strutted confidently out to greet Lyle like some over-sized kingfisher. At his flank was a soldier clutching a halberd. Lyle felt his pulse quicken. The footman held a mask attached to a thin rod, which he lowered to appraise the new arrivals. "Sirs?"

This was the first test of Lyle's nerve, and he held his breath behind his own ostentatious mask of gold and black. It was fastened by a string about the back of his head so that there was no danger of it slipping, and he bowed, the mask's goose feather fringe wafting at his scalp and tickling his ears. "Sir Ardell Early," he said, his voice sounding so peculiar in the muffled confines of the disguise. He glanced over his shoulder at the figure who had accompanied him to the door. "And Winfred Piersall."

The footman considered the names, and for a terrible moment Lyle thought they had been discovered, but the man offered a wide smile and a deep bow and swept his arm back grandly. "Your servant, gentlemen. I hope you enjoy your evening."

The men allowed themselves to be shown into the house's inner sanctum. There would be no further need to prove their credentials, for a masquerade ball was precisely that - a masquerade. Men and women were not themselves on an evening such as this. They were whoever they wished to be, hidden by their disguises and afforded complete anonymity for the night. It was a fashionable pastime on the continent, and would, Lyle suspected, have become quite the thing in England had the Stuart dynasty survived its time of judgement. But now such public displays of opulence, not to mention the private exchanges of carnality that inevitably went on in darkened corridors behind the bright ballrooms, were not condoned by Cromwell and the men, like William Goffe, who ruled in his name. And yet, though theatre had been banned, and many of the great pagan-spawned festivals that had been adopted and adapted by the High Church were doggedly repressed, the new regime understood when it was politic to cool their instinctive censoriousness. Their great supporters - those strongmen who had killed a monarch, purged a Parliament and made Cromwell king in all but name - were occasionally to be allowed down from the giddy moral heights to which they had been thrust. When it served a purpose.

"Your lad did well," Grumm, upholstered in a green suit and mask so that he looked to Lyle like a huge frog, muttered under his breath as they were ushered along a well-lit corridor.

"Pays to know a Little Mercury or three," Lyle replied in hushed tones. The highways and lanes of Hampshire were abuzz in daylight hours with boys and girls around the age of eleven or twelve, delivering letters and invitations from one great house to another. They were the life-blood of rural communities, and Samson Lyle had recognised their worth almost as soon as he had embarked on his criminal crusade. He had several in his pay, who provided him with gossip and occasionally intercepted useful correspondence. In this case, he had asked his contacts to keep their eyes sharp for letters bound for Sir John Hippisley's estate. One lad had brought him two such documents. Both declining invitations to this evening's masquerade. One from a wool merchant known as Sir Ardell Early, the other from Winfred Piersall, a moderately successful goldsmith.

"You think Sir Frederick's here?" Grumm asked.

"Aye," Lyle replied just as quietly. "Goffe wants something from Hippisley. Money or land. This dance is part of the payment. Mason will be here reminding Sir John of his obligations." He noticed the kingfisher-clad footman glance over his shoulder. "I was just saying," he added in a louder voice, "that this place is exquisite."

The footman nodded. "Quite so, sir. Sir John purchased the seat five years ago, yet still he improves upon it. We have a large hall, as you will presently see, two parlours, and twenty-one chambers. There is a brew-house on the estate, along with a malt-house, stables, barns, and our own hop garden." His ears quivered, and Lyle assumed he was smiling behind the mask. "Even a bowling green, would you believe?"

"I look forward to complimenting your master on such a fine home," Lyle said.

They reached the end of the corridor and the footman pushed a set of double doors that opened into a sizable room that might have been used to entertain dinner guests once they had removed themselves from the grand hall. There were tables lined against one wall, crammed with goblets full of various types of liquid, while a small choir of perhaps a dozen children were arranged opposite. They wore white robes and masks, which, to Lyle's eye, made them look like faceless cherubim. Something he found profoundly disturbing. They sang a high, lilting tune that was sweet enough, but did little to assuage his unease. More mirrored doors were on the far side of the room, flanked by a pair of retainers as luxuriously dressed as the rest of the staff, and Lyle guessed they would lead into the main hall. He gazed left and right. This was to be a grand affair; that much was clear. The panelled walls carried a near impossible shimmer, polished to within an inch of the servants' lives no doubt. Every mirror gleamed, every floor tile squeaked its cleanliness beneath every boot heel, and every tapestry had been dusted and straightened in preparation for the most discerning of guests. Lyle was glad he had dressed in his very best finery. Bella had gone to great lengths to scrub his long riding boots and bring his favourite shirt to the whiteness of virgin snow. She had chosen for him a black coat with slashed sleeves that revealed the yellow lining beneath, and, though he had complained of looking like a gigantic hornet, she had insisted that nothing less would do. The brilliance of the newly freshened shirt collar offset the coat nicely, she had said, and, even Lyle could admit, the delicate lace at his cuffs certainly provided a deal of beauty to the ensemble. It was all finished off, of course, by the gold mask, and now, as he and Grumm were shown into the great hall, he thanked God for it. For he stepped into a roiling cauldron of bodies, all immaculately attired, all disguised, and each one an enemy.

The choir song was overwhelmed by louder, jauntier music from the balcony, even as the rest of Lyle's senses were assailed. It was as if Sir John Hippisley had squandered his entire fortune on this one gathering, such was the display of wealth that greeted Lyle's gaze. A vast hall of polished floor and high ceiling, awash with colour, draped in bright tapestries, transformed for the night into a Venetian ballroom that thronged with figures dripping in gold and silver, lace and satin, feathers and fans and pearls. Music played above the incessant chatter, masked men and women danced in the room's centre, laughing and whooping and calling to one another like so many rainbow-fledged birds. The women wore swirling dresses, voluminous and shimmering, while the men were adorned in such gaudy attire that Lyle felt as though he had stepped into a room full of peacocks.

Lyle could not help but laugh at the sight, and he sensed Grumm at his shoulder.

"Strange," he said, comfortable that the din of the dance would obscure his words to all but his friend. "Always considered this kind of thing belonged to the past."

Grumm gave a low snort. "The lofty peaks we are ordered by the good book to scale, are not always attainable. It is man's nature to kick back at the chains of morality once in a while."

"You're in the right of it. I imagine we shan't find any ardent Puritans here." That was the irony of this brave new world, he thought. The Parliamentarian faction had never been unified in search of a republic. Indeed, the vast majority of the old Roundheads - himself included - had enlisted to oust the king's corrupt advisers, not bring down the entire monarchy. Where the Royalists had fought for their king and the status quo, the rebel cause had been one of disparate factions, all brought together through a common enemy. They were not all dour Puritans, but a violent concoction of Presbyterians and Independents, soldiers and merchants, aggrieved aristocrats, rebellious Members of Parliament, and radical commoners seeking to level the very foundations of society. Little wonder, then, that no sooner had the shared enemy been vanquished, the factions began to rupture. They turned upon one another, tearing the hard-won peace to shreds. It had taken two more wars to finish the quarrel, leaving the Independent party supreme and unassailable: Oliver Cromwell its figurehead, the New Modelled Army its muscle. But that meant a great many of the ordinary rebels had never been as sober and pious as their new masters. They had supported a cause that had overtaken them, overwhelmed them, and now many - most, perhaps - yearned for the old days that, though far from perfect, were not as stifling as life under the Major-Generals. They went to chapel, they prayed and fasted, but if ever an opportunity to while away an evening with dance and song presented itself, the people would flock to it like so many months to a flame.

"Not any proper ones," Grumm muttered, his mind evidently in tune with Lyle's. He inched closer. "What do we do now?"

"Find Mason."

"How?"

"He's a sober sort," Lyle replied, hoping he was right. "He'll be plainly dressed by comparison with the majority. And he's run to fat. Shouldn't be too hard to spot."

"Conspicuous by his banality. What if he knows Sir Ardell Early?"

"I'm in disguise. Besides, we took a nicely bulging purse from Early once, if you recall, and he was not too dissimilar to me in height and build."

"Then what?"

"Then I'll get him on his own."

Grumm jabbed him with a sharp elbow. "And *then* what?"

Lyle shrugged. "I'll think of something."

They moved into the crowd, buffeted by sweeping skirts as couples breathlessly whirled past. He noted the smells. Heady perfumes, lavender oil and rose water, all mingling strangely with the sweat and stale tobacco of the men and the smoke of the hearths. He extricated himself from the mad rush of the wide floor and eased through the bodies to the outer wall, where he turned to observe. It was surreal to see such flamboyance in these austere days, and he felt himself smile at the sight. The men at the apex of society, power-brokers like Goffe and Cromwell, would probably endorse this event for reason of political expediency, but the hearts of those that gave them their power - the radical Puritans at Whitehall - would give out on the spot if ever they knew what Cavalier pursuits went on in this far-flung part of their new Godly empire. He found the idea infectiously pleasant. But more than that, more than the idea of human nature pushing past the grey barriers of England's incumbent rulers, Lyle simply enjoyed the spectacle. The women threw back their heads and laughed, their forms elegant and their hair released from the coifs they would wear during the day. The men seemed freer somehow. No longer tethered to the stakes of probity driven into the nation by the Lord Protector and his formidable army. And there were jewels here too, glimmering, glinting garnets and rubies and sapphires. They winked at Lyle, dazzled him, and he beamed back. Because Alice would have loved an evening like this. She would have danced until dawn and burst with the sheer joy of it.

There were warnings too. Soldiers stood sentry at the four corners of the room, and he guessed there would be more patrolling the rest of the house. He steeled himself against the nonchalance such a lavish spectacle could engender. The waters in which he and Grumm paddled were infested with the most dangerous sharks imaginable.

"I'll take my leave," Grumm said after a short while.

Lyle looked across at him. "Aye." He reached for the green-swathed elbow as the old man went to move. "And Eustace? Take care."

"Gah!" Grumm hissed, shrugging him off. In a matter of seconds he had dissolved into the throng.

Samson Lyle remained in position for another hour, observing discreetly from behind his mask. Occasionally folk would nod to him, and he would return the gesture, but there was no challenge, and the grim sentries knew better than to accost Hippisley's guests without due cause. As the evening wore on, the energetic chaos of the early throws had given way to a more relaxed atmosphere. It was convivial, but more languid somehow, the men having drunk their fill of the best claret money could buy and the women resting their dance-worn feet beside the great tables that verily groaned with a feast fit for the old king. And yet of Sir Frederick Mason there was no sign. Lyle scrutinised every guest as they passed, searching for a man with the lawyer's portly frame, but, though a few came close, none matched the description well enough. He became increasingly frustrated, his plans apparently coming to nothing, and he moved away from the main crowd, slipping out through a small side door and into a quiet chamber that had evidently not been intended for use this night, judging by its lack of decoration. On its far side was a door that occasionally swung open to reveal a bustling servant, and he guessed the kitchens or cellars would be somewhere beyond. Another door was located in the wall to his right. It was made of thick oaken timbers, squat and studded, and he presumed it must lead outside. He went to lean against the cold wall, pleased to have found somewhere peaceful in which to gather his thoughts. He swore softly, infuriated by his own miscalculation. He had been certain that Sir Frederick would attend. He slapped his thigh hard in frustration.

"You seem a tad vexed, Sir Ardell."

Lyle spun on his heels, his heart suddenly frantic inside his chest. It was not the unexpected words that had startled him as much as the identity of the speaker. "Colonel Maddocks, I..."

Colonel Francis Maddocks was not in costume, but had nevertheless donned a fine suit for the occasion, one of all black that made him look like a raven caged amongst parrots. He wore a saffron-coloured scarf to denote his allegiance, pristine and bright as it crossed his torso, complete with his family crest at the shoulder. His hair, silver-flecked black like the head of a jackdaw, fell about his shoulders in matted strands, while his grey eyes were bright in the candlelight. His sword and pistol were the marks of a man on duty, charged, Lyle presumed, with the safety of the illustrious guests, but his face creased in a friendly smile as he stooped a touch to stare into Lyle's mask. "It is Sir Ardell Early in there, is it not?"

"Aye, Colonel, it is," Lyle said, forcing calm into his tone as best he could. "How did you...?"

"Oh, the footman pointed you out to me," Maddocks explained. The deep creases at the corners of his eyes became more pronounced. "I know he should not - and believe me when I say that he did not wish to unmask you, so to speak - but I fear I can be persuasive." His brow furrowed slightly. "But how, Sir Ardell, did you know who *I* was?"

"You wear no mask, sir," Lyle replied, confounded.

"But we have never met. Not in person, leastwise."

Sweat prickled at Lyle's neck. His cheeks felt suddenly clammy beneath the black and gold disguise. "Someone mentioned you were here to keep us all safe, Colonel. And you carry weapons at a masque. It is not so taxing to deduce your identity." He let his eyes flicker briefly across Maddocks' shoulder, where the lion roared in black thread. "Your strength brings you fame, sir."

Maddocks shrugged, playing the game of self-deprecation poorly. "Ah, well, it is good to know my services are appreciated." To hide his reddening cheeks, Maddocks turned slightly, showing Lyle to a bench at the far side of the small room. "I must say, I am surprised to find you here, Sir Ardell."

"I am not so dour as you might suppose," Lyle replied cautiously, thinking back to the letters they had found in Mason's possession.

Maddocks laughed as they sat down, white teeth glowing beneath the coarse bristles of his moustache, and raised his palms in supplication. "I meant nothing by it, sir, truly. But since your good lady wife..." he trailed off as awkwardness overtook him.

So Early's wife had died, Lyle thought. He dipped his head. "I have not found pleasure in many things, tis true," he said, for once needing no pretence. He swallowed the lump that had thickened at the back of his throat. "You were looking for me, Colonel?"

Maddocks nodded. "How fares business, sir?"

"Business?"

"It is my business to keep your business safe, Sir Ardell. Major-General Goffe has entrusted me with a mission of great importance. The safety of his supporters across the Downs is paramount to him. I would speak to those I must protect. This evening seemed a good time to introduce myself, though I confess it is difficult."

Lyle took the hint, but tapped a finger against the corner of his feathered mask. "My apologies, Colonel, but I like to maintain the charade at all times. What is the purpose of a masquerade if our faces are exposed? I would not insult our host by removing my guise." He noted Maddocks' disgruntled shrug, allowed himself a tiny smile, and continued. "But I will tell you that business is well, thank you. The trade thrives, I thrive. The hills hereabouts are ideal for pasture."

"And you've received no trouble?"

"Trouble?"

"Bandits, Sir Ardell," Maddocks replied earnestly. "Brigands. Footpads. Call them what you will."

"Vermin."

"Aye, vermin," Maddocks echoed, eyes gleaming as though they belonged to a fox. "To be exterminated."

"Please God."

"They've not harassed your work?"

Lyle paused for effect. "Oh, they have, to be sure. And it's affected my profits, I don't mind telling you." He gazed across the bench at the colonel, imagining what Grumm might say if he knew he were stringing the Mad Ox along in this manner. "One in particular."

Colonel Maddocks sat back, balling his fists. "The Ironside Highwayman."

Lyle nodded. "The same, sir. By God, I shall skin him alive when he is caught. String the knave up by his entrails."

"Not if I catch him first," Maddocks replied darkly.

"Do you think you will?"

The door swung inward suddenly and both men fell silent as a couple bowled in from the ballroom. They seemed to hang off one another like a pair of old soaks outside a tavern, before the woman, resplendent in billowing blue and yellow, took her young companion by

84

the wrist and dragged him through another door and out into the labyrinthine passageways beyond.

"Be sure of it, sir," Maddocks said when the couple's laughter had faded. "It is purely a matter of time." He stood suddenly, issuing a tight bow. "Part of my task is to make myself known to those I am charged to protect, so I am pleased we are now acquainted. But now I must see to the men. One can never be too careful."

"You do not think Lyle will strike tonight, though, Colonel?" Lyle said, staring up at the soldier. "Not here."

"One can never be certain where that villain is concerned." Maddocks blew out his cheeks, wide nostrils flaring. "I am not fond of masquerades, Sir Ardell. In my view, the likes of that young pair," he indicated the far doorway through which the laughing couple had vanished, "are little more than preening popinjays and wanton harlots. The very epitome of that which we fought to eradicate." He offered a weary shrug. "But they are valued by my masters, and I must see that they are left in peace by this nation's less desirable elements. There are those who would steal the very shoes from their feet, let alone the jewels from their fingers and necks."

"It is a rich prize, I readily concede," Lyle replied, labouring his incredulity, "but there is as much cold steel here as warm gold. The Ironside Highwayman is a mongrel of the road. Such a dog would not bite so large a beast, Colonel."

Maddocks gave a rueful smile. "He is no common villain, Sir Ardell. He cares not for mere thievery. His targets are the new elite. The people of the rebellion. Those whose stars rose as the old regime's fell. Men such as Sir John. Men like us. If I were him, I would be sniffing out this place like a fox eyeing the largest hen-house in the land."

Lyle stood, extending a velvet-gloved hand for Maddocks to shake. "He'll not get past the likes of you, sir."

"You flatter me, Sir Ardell."

"You are not to be trifled with, Colonel, and he knows it. And there are others here. Hippisley himself marched with Cromwell, did he not? Hinton Ampner is this night filled with the men who made the rebellion. Won it." Grumm's disapproving face resolved in his mind's eye, and he inwardly smiled, adding, "Heroes all."

"Well it is kind in you to say," Maddocks said, making for the doorway that would take him back to the ballroom. To the surprise of both men, the door burst open before he reached it, through which blundered a tall man draped in voluminous robes the colour of salmon, his face obscured by a long, hooked beak that was studded with nuggets of pink and yellow glass.

"Colonel Maddocks!" the newcomer exclaimed in a loud voice that echoed about the small antechamber. "All is safe and well within our humble walls, I trust?"

Maddocks bowed, deeply this time, his face splitting in an obsequious grin. "Safe and well, Sir John, naturally." He waved a hand in Lyle's direction. "I was just saying as much to Sir Ardell."

Lyle took to his feet. "Sir John Hippisley?"

"Ha!" Hippisley barked, slapping his silken thigh in delight. "Do not indulge me so, Sir Ardell! You know me well enough, despite this infernal beak. Worn at my goodwife's suggestion, and rued every moment since."

Lyle felt his mouth contract around his tongue as the saliva dried to dust. He realised he was holding his breath and forced himself to release it lest it affect his speech. "It is an admirable disguise." He hurriedly dredged what he knew of the wool merchant from the back of his racing mind. "And we are not so well acquainted that I might instantly know your voice. Not yet, least wise. I fear I do not often have cause or need to leave my estates."

Hippisley nodded, the aquiline nose bobbing in a manner that reminded Lyle of a peculiar pink bird he had once seen in a Parisian circus. Though that animal had stood entirely on one of its thin legs, while the one before him seemed to hop excitedly from one to the other. "Quite so, quite so. But I trust our friendship - and our respective business interests - will flourish side by side, Sir Ardell. Tell me, do you enjoy yourself this night? My little soiree is to your liking?"

"I am enjoying myself greatly, Sir John," Lyle said, beginning to relax now that Hippisley seemed content with his identity. "The good colonel was just assuring me of his intent to rid our fine county of that base rogue, Samson Lyle."

Maddocks cleared his throat, bowing as he shuffled backwards. "I will take this moment to excuse myself, gentlemen, if it please you. Patrols to see to, you understand."

"Of course, Colonel Maddocks, of course," Hippisley said gravely, watching the soldier disappear into the great hall. He turned to Lyle when the door had clunked shut in his wake. "I fear he will lose his mind over that man."

"Lyle?"

"The same. Maddocks makes it his life's work to catch the so-called Ironside Highwayman, but I can tell you that bringing Major Lyle to ground will not be easy. He was a renowned fighter. And I hear he became a master swordsman during his time in exile."

Lyle was astounded at the man's familiarity, given the fact that they had never met. "You knew him?"

Hippisley shook his head. "No, but I am acquainted with many of his old friends." He was a big man, broad as well as tall, so that when he leaned forwards conspiratorially it seemed as though a the whole room dimmed. "The story goes that he fought with Henry Ireton - God preserve his eternal soul - in Ireland. Smashing the papists as was his right and his duty before God."

"Amen to that," Lyle intoned.

"Quite so. But I heard that he lost his nerve. Saw one too many death."

Lyle felt instantly sick and he swallowed back the bile that always singed his throat when Ireland was mentioned. One too many death? Whole towns sacked, their people put to the sword. The smell of smoke and sulphur and roasting bodies came to him like a living nightmare. He breathed deeply, the pungent fumes of the masquerade suddenly as fresh as a meadow by comparison. "What happened?" he heard himself say.

"Argued with Ireton, stormed out of camp, made ship back to England," Hippisley said bluntly. "That was in the last weeks of '51. But Ireton's messengers reached the motherland first, and when he arrived he was arrested for desertion. He escaped, of course, and fled to France."

Christ, Lyle thought, but that was a frighteningly succinct description of the gauntlet he had been forced to run. The journey across the Irish Sea had been a vomit-washed hell, the ride from the northwest of England had been wet and cold, and then he had been run to ground and beaten bloody by the men who had been his subordinates until that moment. When finally he had extricated himself from the dank confines of his cell and found the terrified Bella, they had walked barefoot through marsh and over hill, crossed the snowy peaks that formed England's spine, and made it to the coast where they had stowed away in the hold of a cargo ship bound for the continent. They had been shadows of their former selves by then, half-starved, weather-ravaged and trawling the very depths of despair. He swallowed thickly and somehow conjured an amused grunt. "What exquisite irony. An arch rebel forced to cower in France with the last of the Cavaliers. Forced to swerve both sides of the divide."

"Quite so!" Hippisley bellowed happily. "Deserved nothing less."

"He deserved the noose."

The master of the grand estate seemed to appreciate that, for his pink plumage juddered as he laughed, deep brown eyes twinkling above the beak. "One day, please God."

"But why is the rogue back?" Lyle asked, unable to stifle his intrigue at the breadth to which his notoriety had evidently stretched. "Why risk returning? Especially now that Cromwell rules so completely through his major-generals. Is it true that he was done a grievous wrong?"

"Not a bit of it, sir! Soldiers were sent to his estate to the east of here, charged with confiscating the knave's assets. He was a traitor, after all. His goodwife was home." He dropped his voice to a clandestine murmur. "There was an altercation and, I'm sorry to say, she was killed. Trampled by the horses as she tried to keep them at bay. A terrible accident."

In that moment Samson Lyle could have wrung Hippisley's neck as though he were the very bird he portrayed. "Accident, sir?" he said, every ounce of strength poured into restraining his ire. "It sounds like murder."

No sooner had the words left Lyle's mouth than he knew he had overreached himself, for Hippisley's shoulders were suddenly squared like a defensive barricade, his eyes somehow darker. "Does it now?" he retorted coldly, the mirth all gone. "Then I commend you to keep your thoughts to yourself in company such as this. It was ruled an accident."

Lyle took a small rearward step. "My apologies, Sir John. It was wrong of me to suggest."

"Wrong of you to think, Sir Ardell. Suffice to say, however," Hippisley continued, apparently content with the retraction, "that Lyle believes you are right. He returned last year. Rides with two others, one a woman of all things! Both are masked, though he is not. They target members of the ruling class. Judges, soldiers, lawmakers, tax collectors, businessmen, merchants. The common sort love him, as the peasantry are wont to do. William Goffe, as you'd imagine, would rather like to see him dance the Tyburn jig."

"As would I," Lyle intoned gravely.

"Quite so, my good man, quite so." Hippisley clapped his hands together, the big palms slapping loudly despite their covering of kid skin, and he made for the door to the ballroom. "Now, I must not neglect my guests, though I know not who they are behind their guises, and you must come too."

Lyle tensed. "Very kind in you, Sir John, but I would not be such an encumbrance on my gracious host."

"Not a bit of it, sir! You said yourself that you do not often leave your estates. This is the opportunity to meet folk that might be of interest to you. Those of a like mind and mutual interests. This is why I have been permitted to hold such an event, after all."

Lyle could only nod. How could he refuse? And now he would be escorted about the crowd, directed from one foe to the next, each with their own tale of how the Ironside Highwayman had menaced them, how he should be gibbeted on the highest point of Butser Hill as a warning to others. Each man and woman would look into his eyes, and one, he knew, would eventually recognise him. With creeping trepidation he followed the big man into the main hall. People still mingled, chattered, ate, drank, danced and brayed to the high ceiling. A few heads turned to appraise them, eyes glinting with intrigue. He noticed one woman, resplendent in green and silver, took particular interest, her almost black eyes bright within a mask that had been styled to resemble the face of a cat. She held his gaze for a second, the eyes at once unreadable and intense, and it took all his willpower to tear himself away.

"Might I ask, Sir John," he said as he moved in the wake of Hippisley's imposing frame, "if Sir Frederick Mason is here? I have been meaning to speak with him for some time upon a certain matter."

Hippisley paused, turned, drew breath to speak.

"Sir John!" a man exclaimed with startling breathlessness, bursting from the crowd. He was a servant, wearing the ubiquitous kingfisher livery of the house, and his face, uncovered, was flushed and glistening with sweat.

Hippisley swung the long beak on him. "What is it? Well, spit it out, man!"

The servant stared at the floor. "We are running low on the good claret, sir."

For a moment it looked as though Hippisley might explode in rage, but his broad chest suddenly deflated as he sighed in exasperation. "Must I deal with everything myself?" He turned to Lyle. "Forgive me, Sir Ardell. I will return forthwith."

Lyle nodded rapidly, thanking God for His timely intervention. He might have been denied Hippisley's answer, but at least he would avoid the inquisitive gazes. He watched Hippisley stalk away, now alone in a sea of people, the thrum of the dance like waves lapping all around.

Lyle took the opportunity to flee, making for the antechamber from whence they had come. He needed to clear his head, walking straight to the ugly exterior door that he had guessed would open out into the gardens. It was not locked, the bolt sliding back with a deep rattle, and he stepped quickly into the night air.

The area immediately surrounding the house had been landscaped and planted with various kinds of shrubs and bushes. There were several rows of what he guessed to be fruit trees running through the lawns, their branches naked under the moonlight, and a maze of ivy and honeysuckle sprawled over a complex of trellised fences. Beyond that was the high, moss-clothed wall, keeping the garden separate from the rest of the large estate, and Lyle instinctively walked towards it, wanting to be as far from the heady masquerade as possible.

The sounds of the ball faded as he strode into the night. The air was crisp and fresh, chilling his nostrils and throat, making him feel as if he could finally breathe freely. He paced steadily through a miniature orchard of wizened apple trees, the ground slick beneath his boots, until he came to the ivy-woven trellis, moving to the far side so that he could not be observed from the house. There he paused, tilted back his head at the night sky, wondered how best to abort this evening's reckless task now that it had been shown to be borne purely of hubris. The stars winked, mocking him. He removed his mask, worked his jaw to free it of the stifling feeling the disguise had engendered, and blew a warm gust of air through his nostrils. He knew he needed to find Grumm before he could do anything, so, with another steadying breath, he turned.

"I'm surprised you found the time to attend this evening, sir, given your busy schedule," Felicity Mumford said. "Robbing honest folk, and such." She sniffed daintily. "Still, at least you appear to have bathed for this engagement."

"Madam, I..." Lyle spluttered, replacing the mask despite the terrible knowledge that it was all too late.

She grinned. "Fear not, Major Lyle. I had rather hoped I would meet you again. Though I confess I am surprised it is so soon".

"Thank you," Lyle said, lowering the pointless disguise. He stared at her. In her hand was her own mask. It was green and silver, like her dress, the eye holes turned up at the corners in a distinctly feline manner. "You saw me in the hall."

"I did. I knew it was you. Could tell by your eyes." She ran her free hand through hair that had been freed of the coif she had worn when first they met. The gesture mesmerised him. "Who are you supposed to be? I cannot imagine you were invited in person, sir, for where would they send the invitation?"

He laughed at that. "Sir Ardell Early."

She raised a single brow in amusement. "Not a great likeness, though perhaps similar in height. Besides, Sir Ardell is a bore, and not many here would know him."

"That was my hope." He stepped forward a fraction. "Why did you not raise the alarm before? Why not now?"

"My uncle is a vile man, Major. He despises me, I despise him. We must suffer one another, since he is my only living kinsman, but that does not compel me to like him." The corners of her mouth twitched almost imperceptibly. "And I like you. Lord knows why, but I do. I suppose you were kind to me, even as you threatened me with that ghastly pistol you carry." She shuddered, casting her gaze to the grass between them. "But will you tell me the truth?"

"Truth?"

Now she searched his face again, her dark visage illuminated by the warm glow from the house at her back. "They say you ride against the government for the memory of your late wife. Is that really why you turned outlaw?"

He nodded. "Aye. She was murdered in vengeance for my betrayal. Her and my unborn child."

Felicity's fingers went instinctively to her lips. "Oh, Lord. I am sorry, Major. Truly."

He looked away, unable to meet her eye. "No matter." He found himself walking amongst the dense barricades of ivy and honeysuckle. She was with him. "The passage of time serves to numb the pain, if not the fury," he said after a short while. "I have rebuilt my life. Made my money. I am, I suppose, content. But I'll wage my private war until there is no more breath in my lungs."

"And why did you betray them?" she asked tentatively.

"I joined the Parliamentarian struggle when I was a child, Miss Mumford. Served under Cromwell at the age of sixteen at Naseby. A boy before the drums began to beat: a man after they fell silent. Campaigned against all the bitter uprisings of the second war and rode with our newly made force in the third. I saw many terrible things. Too many horrors to number. And yet none of that mattered when we went to Ireland. Women and children.

The infirm, the weak. They were as rodents to us, and we exterminated them as we would a nation of rats. It was no longer war. I decided to ride away. A decision that I have paid for every moment since."

They reached the end of one of the ivy corridors where it met with the sheer face of the high wall. The moonlight was shut out of this corner and it was utterly dark. "Why are you here, Major?" Felicity asked. "It is unimaginably dangerous for you."

He hesitated, wondering whether a confession would be sheer folly. But she had known it was him, and done nothing about it. "I would free a prisoner held by Goffe's men," he said. "Your uncle's strongbox..."

She smirked. "The one you ruined?"

"Aye. It contained a letter mentioning this man. One James Wren. He will be transferred from Newbury to Portsmouth."

"When?"

The sounds of giggling carried to them on the breeze and they both looked round. Nothing came from the darkness. Another couple escaping the crowds.

"That, Miss Mumford, is my difficulty," Lyle said. "It did not indicate when."

"Watch the road," she suggested bluntly.

He shook his head. "Wren was a prominent Cavalier. The guard will be heavy."

She arched an eyebrow. "Too heavy for the great highwayman? Could you not leap out in surprise?"

"Imagine a cat leaping out upon a flock of sparrows, only to discover that they're hawks."

She laughed at that. "So you require time to plan."

He dipped his head. "I need to know when he will be moved. And I had hoped Sir Frederick would attend this evening."

Her jaw dropped. "And you were simply going to ask him?"

"Yes."

She laughed again in the darkness. "You are a strange creature, Major Lyle, that is for certain." Before he realised she had moved, her hand was on his cheek. It was warm and he angled his face, pressing against it. She was so close, though he could only discern her outline in this sepulchral recess of the garden. But he could smell her, and feel her breath.

He inched away. Just a fraction, but enough to break the trance. She was perfect to his eyes, and that knowledge hurt him. Brought guilt crashing through his chest to invade his heart. He thought of Alice.

Then she moved, closing the divide just as he had opened it, climbing to the tips of her toes, and her lips were on his, parting a fraction so that he could feel the lambent tip of her tongue. And then she was gone, stepping away from him as his rushing pulse hammered in his ears.

"He is here," she said. "He does not condone such events, of course, but even dour men like Uncle Frederick concede such frivolity must be allowed on occasion. Hippisley is to be rewarded, for he served the revolution well, and his allegiance must continue to be nurtured. His charisma holds a deal of sway here in the Downs, so says my uncle."

"Where is he?" Lyle managed to say, his mind still clouded by her actions. "Where is Sir Frederick?"

She gave a sharp, bitter chuckle. "Uncle will not dance, or be seen to give it his blessing. But he is here. Put that mask back on, and follow me."

The drawing room was on the far side of the house, looking out onto the front courtyard via a pair of large, rectangular windows that were crammed full of diamond-shaped panes of glass. Samson Lyle waited in the corridor outside, watched with disinterest by a bored looking footman, but he caught a glimpse of the room's interior as Felicity Mumford half-opened the door and bustled in. Lyle watched as she walked, skirts hissing like a chorus of serpents behind, and, just as she disappeared inside, he spotted two familiar faces. One was that of Sir Frederick Mason. He wore no hat, but the rest of his attire had not changed since the robbery. Felicity had said that he disapproved of such events, but Lyle could see that such a claim was a stark understatement, for the sober black coat and plain white shirt were conspicuous in their absence of colour. Mason sat at a large table scattered with papers and scrolls. He studied one intently, not looking up as his niece entered, a quill poised in his right hand. The other man was standing at his shoulder. He wore the attire of a soldier, even donning a breastplate for the occasion, though it was no masquerade costume. Kit Walmsley, Mason's bodyguard, was grim-faced and alert. He looked up immediately upon seeing the door open, one hand reaching for the hilt of his sword, and frowned when he saw that it was her. For a heartbeat his little eyes flickered past her shoulder to stare at the doorway. They met Lyle's gaze, held firm. Walmsley cocked his head to the side like a confused hound as he stared at Lyle, and then the door slammed shut.

Lyle did not know whether to linger or make good his escape. If Walmsley had somehow recognised him, then trouble would be quick on his heels. But he could not afford to flee. He needed to know when the authorities planned to move James Wren, and the chief lawyer to the Major-General of Berkshire, Sussex and Hampshire was the only man who had that information. He had come too far to let the night's efforts go to waste.

A bell tinkled gently from somewhere further down the passageway, and the glum footman trudged away, leaving Lyle alone. He edged closer to the door. The murmur of voices carried to him, muffled and too quiet to discern, but no shouts came forth, no hue and cry was being raised. He held his breath, stepped back. The door handle clicked, light streamed out to illuminate the dull corridor, and there stood Felicity Mumford. She stared hard at him, gave the tiniest shake of her head, and called a friendly farewell over her shoulder. Lyle needed no further encouragement and made to leave. He strode quickly over the polished tiles, footsteps echoing in the confined space. He could sense Felicity walking behind, deliberately slower, and knew she was making out that she was not associated with him. Then he heard a man's voice, deep and authoritative. He recognised it immediately. It was Walmsley.

Lyle cursed viciously and picked up the pace, searching for somewhere in which he might hide. There was some kind of altercation behind, raised voices, a man and a woman, and he knew Walmsley had accosted Felicity. His instinct was to double back, knock the bodyguard onto his rump for speaking to her thus, but knew he could not. He did not even glance round at them, instead reaching the end of the corridor, pushing through a small doorway, and finding himself in a room full of liveried servants. They called to one another angrily, anxiety the common vein through each voice. The room contained a large table at its centre, men and women round the outside, each in position by various work-surfaces. One woman in heavily stained apron stood like a sentinel before an imposing hearth, overseeing a pair of young lads tending the fire. Above the flames, spitting and hissing as teardrops of fat plummeted into the white-hot embers, a pig turned on a spit, its skin darkening from the heat. Lyle realised he was in the kitchens, the very heart of the house, and he recalled that the little antechamber where he had encountered Maddocks and Hippisley was on the far side. He ran now, dispensing with any show of decorum, baffled members of the house staff left slack-jawed in his path.

He passed through to the chamber beyond, pleased to discover it empty and silent. He considered going for the little studded door that would take him into fresh air, but he knew he had to find Grumm. With a pounding heart and twisting guts, Lyle entered the main hall.

The ball went on unhindered, ignorant to his private fear. Lyle plunged into the throng, forced to use more force than he had wanted as he cleared a path, much to the consternation of the revellers. Hands grasped at him, wanting to know why he shoved so rudely, and then he heard the word he dreaded. His name. His real name.

The hall fell silent as one. The musicians up in the gallery ceased as though some mystical conflagration had devoured their instruments in the blink of an eye. He kept going, kept pushing his way through the bodies.

"Lyle!" Kit Walmsley's stentorian voice ripped through the pungent air again. "Samson Lyle! You will halt, damn your eyes!"

And then he knew it was over, for more and more masked faces were looking at him. Those strangely blank expressions examining him as though utterly dispassionate, yet behind the disguises he knew they would be far from disinterested. A few brave souls placed themselves in his path, slowing his flight, then others grasped his shoulders and arms, clawing, dragging. He felt as if he waded through molasses. A huge paw landed hard on his shoulder, wrenched him round, its match grasping at his face until the mask slid free. Silence again. Samson Lyle had been captured, the wolf run to ground. Kit Walmsley's wide, ruddy face grinned back at him as the former Roundhead tossed Lyle's mask away in disgust as though it were a lump of rancid meat. His nose was still swollen, the nostrils scarlet tinged, and his eyes were slung with heavy blue bags.

Lyle's brain raced. The colours and scents and sounds of the evening swirling like storm-harried leaves. Christ, he thought, but it was all over. They had failed. A year of evading - taunting - the authorities had come only to this. A pathetic flash in the pan, his audacious shot at greatness fizzling to nothing, the powder dampened by arrogance.

"I see your snout has yet to recover," Lyle said defiantly.

Walmsley's hand fell to his sword, thick fingers snaking round the grip. The stunned revellers gasped, letting their quarry go so that they might move clear.

Samson Lyle punched the stout old soldier in the face. It was not as hard as it might have been, for he had only time and space for a straight, sharp blow, but Walmsley's recent wounds were fresh and vulnerable, and his nose caved in like a sodden honeycomb. He wailed, the anguished bellow reverberating around the high ceiling as he staggered backwards. He did not fall, but blood spouted freely down his chin and between the fingers that pressed over the damage in a futile attempt to stem the flow and numb the pain. Lyle saw his chance, rushed into Walmsley, shoving him back further with one hand and gripping his sword hilt with the other. The blade rasped free as its owner fell away, and Lyle spun on his heels. The crowd screamed, sheered away from the glittering steel like a flock of sheep in the face of a rabid dog, and a path soon opened up.

"That's two blades you've given me now, Kit!" Lyle called over his shoulder. "You really are a tremendous benefactor!"

Walmsley brayed into his cupped hands. Lyle laughed. The crowd screamed. More shouts erupted as Lyle moved, though this time he recognised them as the soldiers who had been set to guard the room. There would be at least four, he knew, perhaps half a dozen, and each would have a musket. But they would not dare discharge the lethal weapons amongst the packed gathering, and he gauged there might be a few moments to carve a path through to the entrance hall that he remembered from when first he and Grumm had entered.

"Lyle!" another challenge snarled above the panicked din.

Lyle turned to see a familiar face. "Ah, the Mad Ox. Have you enjoyed your evening?" He backed away, the gaudily clad revellers parting like the Red Sea to let him through. "What was it you said? Sir John's guests are little more than preening popinjays and wanton harlots, was it not?"

Colonel Maddocks advanced passed the reeling Walmsley, his face dark with barely restrained fury. He had been duped and he knew it. He did not draw his pistol, for the crowd was too deep and fluid to guarantee their safety if a shot were discharged, but his brutish broadsword was in his hand in the blink of an eye. "You're trapped, Lyle," he said, voice a seething rasp. "Fodder for my hounds."

"We shall see, Ox," Lyle replied as calmly as he possibly could. He had reached the doorway now, and backed into the entrance hall where the choir had earlier sung so sweetly. They were still there, bunched like penned lambs, but now their mouths were shut, eyes wide, faces pale.

The entrance hall was different than Lyle remembered, if only by way of atmosphere. When he and Grumm - Ardell Early and Winfred Piersall - had crossed its polished tiles, the place had been a picture of serenity. The choir chirping like baby birds, the candlelight flickering, the mirrors and tapestries bringing brightness and warmth to the grand stone structure. But now the room was one of bleak horror. The mirrors reflected only stunned faces and sharpened blades. Men, women and children pressed back in a terrified crush against the walls, desperate to be away from those who would brandish cold steel on so merry an occasion.

Lyle ignored the cries and gasps. He was an animal cornered, senses suddenly keen. His enemy stalked into the chamber too. Behind him the revellers were pressing into the doorway from the ballroom, desperate to witness the confrontation unfold, as long as they stayed safely out of range. Maddocks was sneering, swishing his heavy blade out in front, beckoning Lyle onto its tip. He had plenty of courage, Lyle knew well, but no doubt revenge gave the colonel an extra impetus this night. After all, their last meeting had ended in abject humiliation for Maddocks, despite the fact that Lyle had hardly behaved with any chivalry.

Maddocks lunged. He did not have the finesse of Walmsley, but nor did he require it. His tutelage had been gained on the field of battle, and he knew how to fight without the airs and graces of the fencing masters. His arm was extremely strong, the blade a single-edged cavalry sword that was intended for cleaving rather than duelling, and though Lyle parried easily enough, he was forced to give ground simply to avoid being overwhelmed by the sheer power of his old comrade. Lyle jabbed with the blade he had taken from Walmsley, striking out at Maddocks' sword arm, but the colonel was alive to the threat and patted it away.

"I will fight you!" Samson Lyle bellowed, but he did not mean Maddocks. "All of you! Every soul here!" The crowd murmured uneasily.

"You will not fight after this day!" Maddocks spat back. "You have nowhere to go, Lyle! Nowhere to hide!" He glanced about at the assembled faces. "This is Major Samson Lyle. Look upon him. See the fear in his eyes. This is the Ironside Highwayman. Maker of the republic, breaker of oaths. Deserter! Traitor! Outlaw! He has no home but the road. No cause but the memory of a dead wife!"

This time Lyle attacked, thrusting the long rapier at Maddocks' face. The colonel swept away the threat with contemptuous ease, whipping the point of his own sword at Lyle's lower ribs. Lyle parried, flicked his thinner, lighter weapon up in a darting riposte. He felt the point scrape at something, jumped back to assess, and saw that a thin crimson line had been drawn vertically down the centre of Maddocks' wide chin. Maddocks looked stunned. He lifted a hand to the graze, winced as he stared down at bloody fingertips, and a low, guttural growl seeped from his throat.

The colonel lurched forward, fat droplets of blood flinging from his chin to spatter the floor. He slashed the air between them in a series of lightning arcs that threatened to smash through Lyle's defences and eviscerate his chest. Lyle barely had time to react, recoiling and parrying, the shuffle of skirts and feet ever-present as the ring of onlookers surged out of the way. He blocked a low strike, then one from on high, twisted out of range of the next, and felt his back collide with the cold wall. Women screamed on either side as Maddocks advanced, bringing across his blade in a savage horizontal swipe designed to cleave Lyle in half. The highwayman managed to get his own steel in its path, but Walmsley's rapier was no match for the solid weight of the broadsword, and Lyle felt his stomach turn as the thinner blade snapped in two. It was enough to send Maddocks' blow skittering off to the left, beyond Lyle's elbow, and a spray of hot wax showered the side of his face as a fat candle was cut in two. He dropped the useless hilt, hooked an arm around Maddocks' elbow so that the colonel's sword was locked against the wall.

They were inches apart now. "You'll be strung up on the Downs, Lyle," Maddocks rasped as he struggled to wrench his sword arm free, his fetid breath invading Lyle's nostrils. "It is over."

Lyle kicked the soldier hard in the crotch, twirling away as Maddocks cried out. He stared about the open space, searching for a weapon, anything he could use. Out the corner of his eye he caught sight of a man dressed all in green. From behind the green mask, eyes of pale blue glistened. Lyle thanked God, because it was time to leave. "Bella!" he shouted.

Maddocks had straightened. His face was deep red, breathing laboured, his eyes like bright orbs. He still clutched his heavy blade, and he levelled it, the point in line with Lyle's throat.

And someone stepped out from the choir.

Maddocks and Lyle both turned to look at the masked child who had walked into the blood-streaked ring.

"Enough play, Samson," the girl's voice announced. It was a surreal and incongruous sight. A girl clothed all in white, her appearance and tone angelic, yet when she drew her hands from behind her back, they bore objects synonymous with death. She raised both pistols, ugly and black in her grasp. One was pointed at Maddocks, the other swept perpetually back and forth, threatening every soul in the room. "'Bout time we went home, I reckon."

Lyle went to her, feeling Maddocks' gaze like a dagger in his spine. He took one of the pistols, checked that it was cocked, and stretched out his arm. "It has been a wonderful evening," he announced, "and I have thoroughly enjoyed myself. But now it is sadly time to take our leave." A murmur of impotent discontent rustled through the room, like a stinging breeze heralding a storm. He noticed the crowd at the doorway, faces still clamouring for a view of the incident, bodies pushing through to the small chamber from the great hall beyond. Foremost in that pack was the stocky form of Kit Walmsley, his nose a ragged mess. Lyle winked at him, causing the older man to step into the temporary circle as he took the bait like a crazed animal, but a shake of Lyle's pistol halted him just as quickly.

Silence followed. Tension. People were still moving at the entrance to the hall, and Lyle knew that the armed guards must surely be moving through the throng. He glanced over his shoulder. "Ready?"

Eustace Grumm, still masked in green, was standing beneath the lintel of the rear door. "As I'll ever be, you mad fool."

Lyle laughed. He and Bella edged backwards, pistols still poised. The circle of onlookers seemed to contract as they moved, terror at witnessing the fight turning rapidly to rage. A pair of soldiers broke through the crowd, as Lyle had predicted. They each brandished muskets, the wheel-locks wound and ready to fire. Still, though, the risk seemed to deter them. The range was nothing, a matter of yards, but a misfire would kill innocents and they were too timid to take the chance.

"Shoot!" a voice barked suddenly, making the soldiers - and consequently everyone else in the room - flinch violently. "I said shoot the villains, you spineless women!"

Sir Frederick Mason's rotund form waddled into view. He was ruddy faced and furious, spluttering indignantly as he spoke, the veins in his nose raised and livid like a blood-spun cobweb.

At his shoulder another, taller man appeared. He had discarded the salmon-hued beak to reveal a handsome face that was lantern-jawed, with a wide mouth and deep-set eyes. "Hold!" he ordered.

"Why thank you, Sir John," Lyle addressed Hippisley.

The master of the house ignored him, turning instead to Mason. "I'll not have muskets fired in my damned house, Sir Frederick. No, sir, I will not. The safety of my guests is paramount."

"Now, Sir John," Lyle said, "I would ask these men to leave." He nodded at the guards. "Both of you. Back into the hall. Have a dance, perhaps."

The soldiers looked bewildered, uncertain, but Hippisley raised a staying palm. "You will remain." He swung his gaze upon Lyle. "You are trapped, Major Lyle. You cannot possibly hope to make it out of Hinton alive. There are guards everywhere, you fool. Not only these, but at the door. Out in the grounds. You think me a dullard?"

"No, Sir John, not a bit of it. Indeed, that very fact is what has made this night so utterly thrilling."

"Then admit when the game is up. Hand yourself in. No one else need be harmed."

Grumm and Bella were with him, which meant he had no further need to linger, and Lyle took a step rearward, ready to make for the door. The musketeers might shoot when they were out in the open, but he wagered they would not discharge their weapons inside the house. He drew breath to call to his companions. It was worth the gamble. But at the corner of his eye he caught movement. A woman with long, dark hair, dressed in green and silver. She had discarded the mask, and he saw the corners of her mouth twitch upwards as, he had come to learn, they often did when she regarded Samson Lyle. He knew he should just flee while he had the chance, but something in her eyes made him act. He lunged for her. She resisted, screamed. He kissed her hard on the lips, their teeth clinking. She struggled, screamed again.

Sir Frederick Mason stepped forward, his face taut. "Touch her again, you evil filth, and I shall have the skin flayed from your bones!"

"Unhand me, sir!" Felicity Mumford shrieked. The crowd echoed her anguish.

"I'm afraid you're a tad late for that, Sir Freddy," Lyle grinned, and he kissed her again, more softly this time, before spinning her about, pinning her against him with one arm, and lifting the gun to her throat with the other. She twisted as if to resist, but it was not a concerted effort.

"Now, if you'd be so gracious, please remove those ghastly muzzles from such a well-appointed room."

"Sir John," Mason bleated at the renewed threat, his bluster punctured.

"You'll die a criminal's death!" Sir John Hippisley bellowed, but he waved the musketeers away. They melted back into the crowd.

Lyle put his lips to his captive's ear. "Well? What is it?"

"A traitor's death!" Colonel Maddocks, sword still in hand, snarled over the thrum of the guests who were in equal parts appalled and enthralled.

Lyle dragged Felicity away from her uncle, and from Hippisley and Walmsley and Maddocks. Her heels scraped as she lost her footing on the tiles, but he took her weight easily. The crowd shifted to let them through, Grumm holding the doorway, Bella swinging her pistol in warning against any who might think themselves courageous.

Felicity tilted back her head as they moved. Her breath was warm as she whispered. "Three days, Major. At dawn."

"I would kiss you again," Lyle hissed.

"Please do not. I fear it would rather compromise my position."

117

"Thank you. I will come for you, Miss Mumford. I swear it."

"Do not bother, sir. The life of a brigand is hardly something to which I aspire."

"In time, they will know you've told me," Lyle said as they reached the doorway. "What will happen to…?"

"Me?" she cut in. "I can deal with Uncle Frederick, do not worry."

Lyle stared at their pursuers. "Have the dowdy wench, Sir Freddy!" He released her, slapping her rump hard as she bolted back into the room. She yelped in exaggerated outrage. He laughed. "I grow tired of her already!"

Lyle, Bella and Grumm raced along the passageway through which they had earlier been conveyed, the small flames of candles guttering madly as they rushed past. There were a couple of footmen in their way, shimmering in their red and blue suits, but they did nothing in the face of the armed fugitives, instead pressing themselves tight against the timber clad walls to allow the trio through. Bella was laughing, high-pitched and giddy with excitement. Grumm was cursing their collective stupidity, though Lyle wagered he would be grinning behind his mask. They knew a pursuit would already be underway, Maddocks and his men charging out of the mirrored chamber like a herd of stampeding heifers, but they were already at the large porch, the door open, stars pricking the black sky beyond.

"Took your time," Lyle called as they burst out into the fresh night.

Grumm ripped off his mask, tossing it into one of the shrubs that lined the path along which they ran. "There were eight, Major. Eight o' the buggers to gather. Not easy, I can tell you."

"But you succeeded?"

"I'd have told you by now if I hadn't, you beef-witted lump."

Lyle eased his pistol's pan cover closed, thrust it into his belt, and clapped Grumm between the shoulders. "You're a grand fellow, Eustace!"

Shouts rang out behind. Lyle glanced back to see a score of men pour out from the manor house. "How far?"

"See for yourself," Grumm rasped.

Sure enough, as they passed a stand of ancient elms, the three came to a small clearing. The main high road lay just beyond, but before that, tethered loosely beneath the branches of a soaring ash, were Star, Tyrannous and Newt. The horses looked up from their grazing, whickering gently as they recognised their respective keepers.

Star snorted irritably when Lyle untied the reins and leapt into the saddle. The big grey evidently sensed the urgency in his master's actions, and Lyle stroked the beast's thick neck, praying there would be no panic this time.

Shots split the night. The trio flinched, ducked down, though the musketeers would be too far away for the range to be effective. "Calm, boy, calm," Lyle murmured softly into Star's sharp ear. He straightened, looked across at Grumm. "What did you do with them?"

Grumm grinned, his face a rictus of wolfish pride and sharp, crooked teeth, as he pointed away to his left. "There. Took an age to get 'em comfy enough to share my wine."

Eustace Grumm had been chief of a complex ring of smugglers in his native Cornwall. He had used intimidation, poison, steel and guile to outwit his rivals and the Customs men alike. But after a rival had tipped them off as to his whereabouts one balmy night a year after the First Civil War had reached its bloody conclusion, he had barely escaped England with his life. He spent the following years living as a vagrant on the Continent, frightened and destitute. Surviving off scraps discarded by the kitchens of the great town houses of

Calais, stealing when he could, and spending much of his time existing in the shadows, evading the thief-takers who lurked in his wake. And then, on the road south to Paris, the lawmen had caught up with him. They found him in a busy coaching inn, beat him and dragged him outside, the noose already slung over the bough of a stooped tree.

But a man named Samson Lyle had been in that same tavern. He had watched quietly from the within the fug of tobacco smoke as questions had become quarrel, and quarrel had become arrest. And as the five thief-takers had laughed their way out to the place of summary execution, that silent, watchful man had appeared in the night air, double-barrelled pistol in one hand, blade in the other, and he had prized Eustace Grumm from their clutches. The old man had latched onto him like a limpet after that. Riding with him through northern France, providing the former cavalry officer and his young ward with companionship and laughter, while his expertise in the ways of the outlaw had often proved invaluable. Indeed, thought Lyle as he squinted into the inky darkness to discern the row of eight prone bodies that had been left at the foot of one of Sir John Hippisley's trees, the irascible old criminal possessed knowledge that extended far beyond contraband. He looked up from the row of saffron-scarfed soldiers as more guns spat their fury from the direction of the house. "Just wine?"

Grumm's face twisted in its ugly tick. "And a sprinkle o' certain mushrooms."

"You are a marvel, Mister Grumm."

"Thank you, Major Lyle," Grumm replied as they kicked hard at the mounts.

"They ain't dead, are they?" Bella asked.

"No, lass," Grumm replied, loudly now above the crash of hooves and crackle of musketry. "But they'll have sore skulls in the mornin', I promise you that!"

PART THREE: THE BRIDGE

Near Liphook, Hampshire, December 1655

The driver's name was Tomkin Dome. He was not yet fifty, but he knew his days were numbered. He could feel it, feel the burn in his chest with every breath, the innate brittleness in his bones. He could taste the acrid mucus he hawked clear of his throat each morning, certain it had become tainted. And his skin. God, but it itched. Gnawed at him during the night like an army of rats, pus-filled boils forming on his forearms and face, livid and moist. The jangling of the cart did not help matters. Every judder and jerk made a patch of corrupt skin sear with pain, or burst, soaking his clothes with stinking moisture. Christ, but he hated his life.

He took a flask of wine from a small bag beside him on the seat and pulled out the stopper with his teeth. When the liquid burned his throat, he closed his eyes, finding happiness only in its richness. He had tasted better, of course. Back before the rebellion, in the good times, when his trade in Lymington and Hayling sea salt had thrived and he could afford the very best that life had to offer. But then the wars had come, and Tomkin Dome had pinned his colours to the wrong mast. Now he had nothing but a waggon to his name, bitterness in his heart, and relentless, grinding agony.

Dome thrust the flask home and squinted into the murky dawn. It was close upon eight o'clock. A thin mist crept up off the River Wey to extend white fingers between ancient boughs and over the wide road. Grey clouds, pregnant and vast, loomed ominously overhead. The air smelled of rain. There was no breeze so the trees were still, darkening the land either side of the highway, their branches, mostly stripped of leaves, straining for the sky like so many talons. A boil smarted on his rump and Dome shifted his skinny frame irritably, spewing a savage oath as he did so. One of the riders out in front turned back to admonish him in clipped tones. Dome's seething retort was lost, he hoped, amongst the sound of hooves, and he turned his attention back to the job at hand.

The cart was small in size. Not the massive, gilt coaches of the rich and powerful, but an unprepossessing vehicle, plain and functional. It was drawn by a pair of strong horses, a chestnut and a grey, the traces jangling behind as wheels creaked and bounced noisily. The cart had been agrarian in nature at one time, flat and open for grain or

124

hay, but now it was a perfect box, for a metal frame had been placed upon its rear platform, like a giant aviary, with a small door against which a heavy lock clanged. Within the cage, slumped against the bars and swaying with the motion of the vehicle, was a figure. His hair was long, unkempt, framing a face that was bowed from view, as though dipped in prayer. Occasionally the horsemen would call to him. There were ten of them; five out front, five at the rear, and they would make sport of taunting the captive, sneering when he ignored them, laughing when the gaunt, stubble-shaded face deigned to look up.

"Steady!" Tomkin Dome snarled as the horses rounded a kink in the road and approached a small stone bridge. "I said steady, you flea-bit buggers!" He received a host of withering glances from the pious troopers for his trouble.

The cart slowed to walking speed. The vanguard of horsemen - heavily armed harquebusiers - trotted forth first, clattering onto the stone slabs that spanned the Wey. Below them the water meandered lazily. The river was deep here, clear as crystal so that the grey silhouettes of fish could be seen darting in the shadows cast by the grassy banks and amongst the gauntlet of smooth rocks and straggly weeds.

Dome scratched at an ulcer beneath his armpit as he waited for the troopers to wave him on. He was a frail man, given to feeling the cold more than most, but his brow prickled with sweat nevertheless. He drew a cloth from his sleeve, mopping his face. "Well?"

The troopers had gathered at the centre of the bridge. One of them was speaking, but not to the driver. Dome looked past him to see a lone man on the far bank. He looked, to Dome's poor eyes at least, like a scarecrow. A thin, gaunt, crook-backed bag of bones, white-bearded and deeply wrinkled, a filthy bandage wrapped round his skull to cover what was left of an eye lost long ago. The scarecrow seemed to whisper to himself, admonish himself. He would suddenly bellow a scrap of scripture, arguing with some unseen spectre. Occasionally he would twitch, his neck convulsing, one cheek jerking hard as though tugged by an invisible rope.

Tomkin Dome stood. "Long way to go yet, Lieutenant Chickering!"

The most advanced rider twisted in his saddle, his face taut behind the trio if vertical bars that hung from the hinged visor of his helmet. "I am aware of that, Master Dome," he replied testily. "I shall move this doltish beggar off the bridge and we'll be on our way."

126

The scarecrow shuffled forward a couple of paces. "Doltish, sirrah? No, sirrah! Not I! Not ever!"

Lieutenant Chickering drew his sword, leaned to the side so that his saddle creaked. "No further, old man, I'm warning you. Move off the bridge or I'll move you myself."

Tomkin Dome sniffed hard, feeling mucus bubble into his throat. He hawked it up and spat onto the grass at the road's verge. "Enough o' this, Lieutenant. Run the bastard through, or trample him or boot him into the river. I care not, sir, but we must be off." He lashed his horses with the reins and they lurched forth, clattering up onto the bridge. Behind him he could hear the five troopers follow. But Chickering could not move for the scarecrow remained steadfast, gibbering at the dark clouds and dancing a mad little jig, and the young lieutenant seemed unwilling to follow Dome's ruthless advice.

Tomkin Dome laughed heartily, despite his various pains, because he knew Chickering was a kind man at heart, too pious for his own good, and that meant he was stuck for at least the time it would take to dismount and forcibly remove the old vagrant from their path. He did so just as Dome steered his cart up to the apex of the bridge, the rear-guard trotting blithely in his wake, so that the vehicle and all ten of its escort were crammed on the smooth stones above the gargling water.

A pistol appeared in each of the scarecrow's hands.

Chickering seemed to be half dozing, for he did not react for several moments. Eventually he stepped back a pace, jaw lolling, as he absorbed the implication. "Wh... what the devil?"

The scarecrow straightened, losing the curvature in his hunched spine as though a miracle had been performed. He brandished a crooked grin. "Don't do anythin' silly now, me old cuffin. Ground your arms, get your men off their nags, and point to those angry-looking clouds, if you please."

Chickering was a young man, and rolled his shoulders to affect a bluff courage, but the delicate whiskers of his upper lip quivered ever so slightly. "We are ten men, sir."

The scarecrow's blue gaze flickered between the officer and the men mounted at his back. "Ten finely appointed fellows, sir. Shiny armour and pretty weapons. Which of you thinks he might prime his pistol before I stick a bullet twixt his eyes?" No one moved. The scarecrow spat bubbling saliva through the gap in his front teeth. He trained one of the pistols on the lieutenant's crotch. "No plate there, I'd imagine. Now ground arms, you ballock-brained maggot, less'n I turn your cock to a cunny."

"Why you treacherous cur!" Chickering hissed, but he dropped his sword nonetheless. His pistols were holstered in his saddle, too far away to be of use, but he still turned to order the troopers to discard their own.

The scarecrow broke into his little jig once more. "Poor old crump-back! Crazed as a headless cockerel! You might be more respectful o' your elders in future, son."

Up on the cart, Tomkin Dome felt his heart race and he wondered if he would expire there and then. He heard hooves and murmurs behind, and turned, expecting to see Chickering's rear-guard following the order, but they had yet to relinquish their arms.

"Oh God," he whispered, understanding that resistance would catch him firmly in the cross-fire. Then out of the mist came a grey stallion. Its head resolved first, eyes bulging and wild above a diamond-shaped patch of pristine white, steam pulsing in roiling jets from nostrils flared black. It seemed to Dome like a ghoul rising from the very bowels of hell, a snorting demon come to claim souls for torment. He shuddered at the thought, but knew it was no spectre, for a man emerged from the wisps, perched atop the beast. He was dressed in dark clothes with a cloak of mossy green, reins in one hand, a curious double-barrelled pistol in the other. The man's face was sharp and lean, the deep lines at cheeks and brow making a once handsome appearance craggy like a sea-smashed cliff. But there was brightness too. In the green eyes, almost glimmering below the brim of his black hat, twinkling from the miasma like lonely stars on a cloudy night.

Dome stood on his rickety timber platform and pointed at the newcomer. "Might wish to check your backs."

The five troopers behind the cart twisted as one. All at once the horses were still. They were trapped on the bridge between two shooters. Yet still they had the superior numbers, and a mad rush at the brigands would certainly sweep them away. Dome swallowed hard, wondering if the soldiers were weighing up their chances.

As if reading their minds, the newcomer let his ghostly grey lope up to the bridge. "This pistol has two shots," he called. "My friend has two also. Fight if you must, but be certain some of you will perish." He lifted a gloved hand to push a tendril of matted sandy-coloured hair from his eye. "Drop your weapons. I will not ask again."

The troopers did as they were told, dismounting and filing up the side of the cart to join their comrades. The cloaked man remained in his saddle, watching from on high, while the scarecrow corralled them like armoured sheep, impotent in the face of the elderly footpad's wolfish delight.

"You," the man in black said, green eyes darting to the waggon.

Tomkin Dome touched a hand to his breast. "Me?"

"Get down and collect the weapons. Toss them in the river."

Dome dropped his reins and scrambled down to the smooth stones. "Aye, sir."

"Then be rid of their mounts, save two."

Dome nodded, already cradling three swords, a pair of pistols and a carbine. "Right away, sir."

As he scurried about his work, he saw that the scarecrow was jabbing his twin pistols in the faces of the soldiers. "Over there, and be quick about it," he ordered, forcing them back against the side of the bridge. "Any one o' you makes a move, you'll get a ball in the throat." He looked between them at the crystal water. "Or maybe I'll save the lead and shove you straight into the drink. Pretty deep, ain't it? Wonder how well you'll swim with all that plate weighin' you down."

"Cover yourself, Eustace," the man perched on the big grey called.

The scarecrow screwed up his face. "They've seen me."

"They've seen a haggard old man. Give them no more to recall than that."

Reluctantly, and with a spiteful sneer, the scarecrow tore away his eye bandage and pulled a black cloth over the lower portion of his face. Chickering bristled, his own features crimson with rage. "You won't get away with this." He glanced across at the mounted assailant. "You'll swing. Both of you."

"Both?" a new voice startled the lieutenant. It was high pitched, the tone of one very young, though it came from the river.

Chickering's eyes widened, as if the speaker were some kind of mythical creature, a nymph dwelling amongst the reeds. The scarecrow grinned and nodded, encouraging the troopers to look down at the water. When the lieutenant turned back, his face was a picture of bewilderment. "A girl? What kind o' highwayman brings his slattern on the road?"

Tomkin Dome had an armful of weaponry, and he staggered to the side of the bridge and dropped them into the glistening depths. He saw her, then. Her face was covered in a silken scarf, but her long hair cascaded over her shoulders to the base of her spine. She too held a pistol, but it was what her other hand clutched that interested him. The girl held a pair of ropes, each taut as they stretched out into the centre of the Wey. Bobbing at their far ends were two small skiffs. She looked up at the bridge. "Get down here, piss-a-breech. And I ain't no slattern. Not any more, least wise."

The scarecrow cackled. "You heard her," he said to Chickering. "Off for a nice trip down the river."

The mounted man walked his horse up to stand beside the cart. He gazed down at the cage, then at Dome. "Do you have the key?"

Tomkin Dome shook his head. "Alas, no, Major. The key is at Portsmouth. None here may open it."

Lieutenant Chickering had been trudging at the head of his men towards the far bank and waiting boats, but now he froze. He turned slowly back, eyes settling on the carter in a look of blazing malice. "You? You have betrayed us?"

Tomkin Dome's entire body hurt. His lungs felt weak and sore, his skin crawled. But he managed a deep bow in spite of it all. "I am a loyal subject of King Charles. And his murdered father before that."

"You will die too, you pathetic little worm," Chickering said darkly.

"I embrace it, young man, for I have taken this small revenge and will die happy." He turned to look up at the horseman. "Thank you."

Major Samson Lyle nodded and slid from his horse. Star grumbled, but kept calm enough. He thanked God for His providence, for the plan had worked. The party had left Newbury on time, and Bella had tracked them so that he knew when they were likely to cross the River Wey. He felt so alive, his blood zinged through his limbs in a way that it had not done since before Ireland. He thought of Felicity Mumford, and, for the first time, felt no guilt.

Lyle reached for one of the saddle's leather loops, through which hung a long war hammer. They were designed for piercing or crushing plate armour, though he had used it against many an infantryman, and the effects on an unprotected skull had been more horrific than he could ever have imagined. Now, though, the target was not skin and bone. It was the heavy lock that hung from the doorway to the cage. Lyle lifted the hammer, poised to strike. "See to our friends, Eustace!"

"Pleasure, Major!" Grumm called back. The old man jerked his pistols and the prisoners resumed their slippery progress down to the grassy bank. "Couple o' nice, cosy boats for you to try, chums," he chirped at the backs of the crestfallen troopers. "Perfectly river worthy I assure you."

Lyle swept the war hammer into the waiting lock. It clanged, the sound echoing about the trees with unnatural loudness, the gurgling of the river its only competition. He repeated the blow twice more with deep grunts, the flapping of startled birds shaking the canopy above, and then there was an almighty crack as the lock twisted and broke. Lyle slid the bolt back, tugged open the door. "Sir James Wren?"

The man in the cage had barely reacted to the frenetic action swirling around him, but now he crawled stiffly to the little doorway. "Aye."

"Then come. The coast awaits. You must take a ship."

Wren took Lyle's proffered hand, bracing himself against it as he stepped out. His hair was lank and filthy, falling over his face in greasy clumps. His eyes stared out from behind the dark veil. He seemed exhausted, broken, though a new light came into his face, as though waking from a terrible dream. "I know you."

"Lyle."

Wren seemed puzzled. "A Roundhead, were you not?"

"I was."

"Allied now to the king?"

"Allied to none but myself."

It was Wren's turn to extend his hand. "I shall tell the king of your service nevertheless."

"As you wish."

Tomkin Dome had chased off eight of the troopers' mounts. Now he came to stand before the man who had hitherto been a captive of the Protectorate. "Sir."

Wren stared at him for a few heartbeats, before his eyes widened. "Sergeant? Sergeant Dome?"

Dome beamed. "You have it, sir, and good it is to see you again."

They shook hands. Wren swept the hair from his face, the life pouring into him with every moment. "What risk you have taken in this enterprise."

Dome's face became sad, and Lyle thought of their first meeting, when the brittle carter had told him of his illness. It had been a Godsend for the mission, but that did not make him happy. Dome cleared his throat awkwardly. "I am not long for this world, Sir James. I would fight for my king one last time." He glanced at Lyle. "Thanks to this man."

Lyle could not stifle a smile. "A small matter, gentlemen. Now if you wouldn't mind, I must be away from here. And you have a ship to catch."

"How?" Wren said.

"The major has arranged our passage to France," replied Dome. "We must ride hard for the coast."

Lyle nodded. "Ride like devils, for they will hunt you."

Wren was already walking gingerly towards the two mounts Dome had selected for their journey, but he looked back at his rescuer. "Why are you doing this, Major? You were a rebel."

"It will hurt Goffe and Cromwell, Sir James," Lyle said as he watched the two men hoist themselves into the saddles and quickly kick the beasts into a canter. The hooves clattered south over the bridge. "That is enough!"

Lyle went to the side of the bridge. He leaned over the stonework to peer down at the two skiffs. They each carried five passengers, fury etched into every face. He waved. "Give my regards to Major-General Goffe!"

Lieutenant Chickering tried to stand, causing the boat to list violently, throwing him back onto his rump. "He will track you down," he snarled as Lyle, Grumm and Bella brayed to the scudding clouds at his floundering.

"I count on it! Be sure to tell General Goffe who it was that outwitted him."

Chickering stared up at him as the boats slipped swiftly downstream. "Then who are you?"

"Major Samson Lyle, sir. The Ironside Highwayman!"

Historical Note

The Rule of the Major-Generals was a 15 month period of direct military government during Oliver Cromwell's Protectorate.

The new system was commissioned in October 1655 and the country divided into 12 regions, each governed by a Major-General who was answerable only to the Lord Protector. The first duty of the Major-Generals was to maintain security by suppressing unlawful assemblies, disarming Royalists and apprehending thieves, robbers and highwaymen. To assist them in this work, they were authorised to raise their own militias.

Colonel Maddocks and his men are figments of my imagination, but William Goffe was indeed Major-General for Berkshire, Sussex and Hampshire, and it would have been his responsibility to hunt down Samson Lyle and men like him.

Sadly, Lyle himself is a fictional character, but he is indicative of many outlaws of the period.

Contrary to the classic tradition of the 18th Century dandy highwayman, mounted bandits have infested England's major roads for hundreds of years.

Indeed, in 1572 Thomas Wilson wrote a dialogue in which one character commented that in England, highway robbers were likely to be admired for their courage, while another suggested that a penchant for robbery was one of the Englishman's besetting sins.

During the years immediately following the Civil Wars, highway banditry became more widespread simply due to the sheer number of dispossessed, heavily armed and vengeful former Royalists on the roads. This idea was the inspiration behind *Highwayman: Ironside*, though I felt it might be more interesting if my protagonist had been a Roundhead rather than a Cavalier.

The locations in the story are all real. The London to Portsmouth road became a major coaching route in the eighteenth century, but it had already been an established highway for centuries. Many inns punctuated the route, and the Red Lion at Rake (now a private house) was certainly present in 1655.

The Manor House at Hinton Ampner was indeed purchased by the Parliamentarian, Sir John Hippisley after the wars. The current house was built in 1790, and is now owned by the National Trust.

The Ironside Highwayman will ride again.

16082211R00080

Printed in Great Britain
by Amazon